UNYIELDING

World War II Trilogy, Book 2

Marion Kummerow

Marion's Newsletter

Sign up for my newsletter to receive exclusive background information and be the first one to know when Book 3 is released.

http://kummerow.info/newsletter

Table of Contents

Chapter 1

October 24, 1936

"Do you, Wilhelm Quedlin, want to take the here present Hildegard Dremmer as your legal wife? Then answer with 'Yes.'"

Hilde looked striking in her knee-length dress, the accentuated waistline hugging her figure to perfection. The red fabric with the white polka dots contrasted nicely with her bright blue eyes while her light brown hair gently brushed her shoulders. But Q didn't have much time to admire the woman he loved.

"Yes, I do," he said, his firm voice underscoring his certainty.

The marriage registrar turned to look at Hilde and asked the same question, "Do you, Hildegard Dremmer, want to take the here present Wilhelm Quedlin as your legal husband? Then answer with 'Yes.'"

"Yes, I do," she responded, absolutely glowing as she smiled at the man she loved. In her smile, he could see the tension of the last year resolve. Sometimes it had seemed they'd never succeed, but they did it. They were seconds away from being married.

"Herewith I declare you husband and wife according to German law. You may exchange the rings now."

Erika stood from her seat and delivered the rings. Q had bought matching wedding bands, but unlike his own, Hilde's ring sported a beautiful princess cut diamond.

After exchanging the rings, the official congratulated them and smiled. "You may now kiss your bride."

Who could resist such a proposal? Q took Hilde into his arms and kissed her lips until she squirmed in his embrace and the witnesses, Erika and Gertrud, clapped their hands.

Q and Hilde, as well as the two witnesses, signed the marriage register, and less than fifteen minutes after they walked into the sober room, the ceremony was over.

Apart from the two obligatory witnesses, no other guests were present. While Q himself was actually glad that the civil marriage ceremony had taken place without foolish emotionalism and pathos, he knew Hilde had wanted something more personal.

He leaned over to whisper into Hilde's ear. "I'm sorry you didn't get the big wedding you originally planned."

Hilde shook her head, a soft smile appearing on her face. "I don't need a big wedding. I just need to be your wife."

Q laughed. "That has been a problem, hasn't it?"

They'd been trying to make this day happen for more than a year, hunting down the paperwork and wading through a sea of red tape in order to receive a marriage license.

Hilde's friends congratulated them, and Q nodded in their direction. "Shall we, ladies?"

He helped all of them into their coats, and once more, his eyes rested on Hilde, who looked absolutely stunning in her pale green woolen coat with three huge wooden buttons.

Hilde and her two friends had chosen everyday clothing. Once they'd decided on a clandestine wedding, they wanted to make it as low-key as possible. Part of the plan was to evade the bevy of photographers waiting outside the registry office to take – and sell – pictures of the bridal couples and the wedding parties.

"Ready?" Q asked, and when they all nodded, he held the door open for the three women, following them outside. It was a nice day with blue skies and just a bite of impending winter in the air.

The photographers immediately gathered around them, raising their cameras, but looked confused when they couldn't make out which woman was the bride. Q reached out and slipped his arms through both Erika's and Gertrud's, and the three of them made silly faces. Moments later, Hilde took Erika's place.

They continued to work their way past the photographers asking them to stop and pose. Q couldn't resist taunting them and asked, "No pictures, boys?"

"Who's the bride?" one of them shot back.

"Wouldn't you like to know?" Q answered with a chuckle. He knew the photographers were there to earn money, but too often, their pictures appeared in the gossip column of the local newspaper. Q shuddered at the thought of being so blatantly displayed. Long ago, he and Hilde decided to keep a low profile, and that included not showing up in the papers.

The photographers finally gave up, moving out of their way and continuing to the next, more willing, bridal party.

Hilde and Q waved goodbye to Erika and Gertrud, who needed to get back to work.

"We'll see you tonight at the restaurant," Hilde added before slipping her arm around Q.

"Mrs. Quedlin," he said, giving her a little wink. "I need a coffee and a pastry to recover from the stress of getting married. What about you?"

She giggled in response and let him lead her the fifteen-minute walk to a pastry shop near their new apartment.

They ordered freshly brewed coffee and two sinfully sweet cream cakes. Hilde's with egg liqueur, Q's with chocolate.

"Aren't you sad that your mother and your friends couldn't attend the ceremony?" Hilde asked him.

Q frowned for a moment before answering, "Sure. I wish Mother could have been present, but she's so fragile lately, I didn't want to make her travel across Berlin for such a short ceremony. We'll visit her next week and take some nice pastry to celebrate." He squeezed Hilde's hand. "For me, the ceremony in itself wasn't important. It was an administrative deed – nothing more. I'm just glad it's over, and you're mine now."

He grinned at her and lifted her hand to his lips, kissing his way up to her elbow. Hilde's cheeks took on a rosy hue, and she quickly removed her hand from his grasp. "Yes, the preparations were tedious, and more than once I thought we'd never be allowed to get married."

"I'm still at a loss at how Gunther managed to finally receive our grandmother's baptism certificate from the priest in Hungary," Q said, smiling at the memory of how hard his brother worked to get that precious slip of paper.

"He really went above and beyond to help us, " she agreed.

"I have a surprise for you," Q said as they finished their coffee and pastry.

"What is it?" Hilde's eyes glowed as she asked, glancing once more at the precious ring on her right hand.

"Jakob asked one of his friends, who is an interior designer, to open up his warehouse for us this afternoon. He has a new shipment of furniture that we can look at."

Hilde pouted, but there was amusement in the gesture. "I still have to get used to your idea of being romantic, but it's a great idea. A comfortable couch would be rather nice."

While Q had moved into their new apartment in the district of Charlottenburg a while ago, Hilde had done so only this morning before going to the registry office.

"Let's go then," he said, once again surprised at her different way of thinking. Hadn't she always complained that the apartment wasn't properly furnished, and the front room contained nothing more than two wooden chairs, borrowed from the kitchen table? So what could be more appropriate than buying furniture on their wedding day?

They had a lot of fun looking at and test-sitting the selection, and after an hour, they purchased two couches and arranged to have them delivered the next day. Jacob's friend congratulated them on their choice of the studio couches. "Well done, my friends. Those are the last high-quality cover fabrics our Fatherland used to make."

Q raised an eyebrow. "How so?"

"Nowadays, all we get are b-grade quality fabrics. The good ones are reserved for military purposes."

Hilde wrinkled her nose. Nobody wanted to believe in the imminence of another war, but the signs became more prominent with every passing day.

Q thanked Jacob's friend once again for the generous offer to buy the couches at a nice discount and then he and Hilde walked back to their apartment.

Hilde had visited the market first thing that morning. Now she removed plates containing cold meats and cheese from the refrigerator. She retrieved the rolls she had purchased as well as some mustard and a small plate of sliced vegetables, while Q set the table for two.

It was a sight to behold, his beautiful *wife* in the kitchen of the apartment that was now their common home.

"I still can't believe we're finally married, Mrs. Quedlin," he said and kissed her lips. They sat at the kitchen table and ate a cold lunch, feeding one another small bites from time to time. They'd meet a few of their best friends later for a celebratory dinner, but that wasn't for hours yet.

And Q already had plans on how to spend those hours. Once it looked like Hilde had eaten her fill, he scooted his chair back and swept her up into his arms.

"Q! What are you doing?" she asked with a laughing shriek.

He paused for a moment and looked down into her blue eyes. "Are we, or are we not, now legally married?"

She looped her arms around his neck. "We are."

Q nodded and carried her towards the bedroom, pushing the door shut behind them with his foot. "Good. Let's act like it then."

***

Several hours later and long into the afternoon, Q blinked his eyes open, stretching his arms above his head. Then he turned his head, kissing the tousled hair of a soundly sleeping Hilde. *I'm a married man.* The mere thought constricted his heart, and he wondered if any man on earth could be happier than him. He'd known he loved her since the first moment he met her two years ago, but actually being married felt different.

She smiled in her sleep, and he couldn't resist stroking her light brown hair, her bare white shoulders, and then trailed a finger down her back. Hilde stirred, but wouldn't wake. When he kissed her on the lips, she murmured something, but still wouldn't open her eyes. A warm feeling took possession of him. *She's mine. And she's the best life companion I could have wished for.*

"Time to wake up, love."

Hilde's eyes fluttered open, a cute blush covering her cheeks as reality settled in. "Hmm, this is how married couples spend their days?" she asked, returning his kiss.

Q grinned. "Since this is the first time I've been married, I tend to believe it is."

"Isn't it wonderful?" She asked and snuggled up closer.

"You are wonderful, my love. I have loved you before, but now it feels like you took total possession of my life, body, and soul."

Hilde giggled. "Wow, that's an unusual statement for a scientist."

Q shifted slightly, furrowing his brows. "I can't explain it. The mere act of signing a paper shouldn't have made any difference to my emotional state, but it did. For some odd reason, I love you even more now, Mrs. Quedlin."

"And I like the sound of Mrs. Quedlin," she said and turned in his arms. Through the window, they saw the sun standing low behind a tree, painting like an artist highlights in the most spectacular forms and colors on the white wall opposite the window. Circles in yellow hues alternated with oval-shaped grey shadows and bright orange patterns that resembled an abstract painting.

"What time is it?" Hilde asked after watching the spectacle for a few minutes.

Q took a look at his watch on the nightstand. "Five-thirty. We probably should hurry up, or we'll miss our own wedding celebration."

Hilde sat up, the sheet slipping down her body. "Five-thirty! We slept all afternoon?"

"Hmm, I remember we did more than just sleep." The fine blonde hairs on her arms stood on end, and he almost regretted that they needed to attend their own wedding celebration. He kissed her bare back. "Go get dressed. I'll use the bathroom after you."

Forty-five minutes later, she stepped into the front room, wearing the same figure-hugging red dress with white polka dots she'd donned earlier that morning, but starring matching red five-inch strappy heels instead of the flat ballerinas. Her tousled hair was carefully combed back into a banana updo, and her face was primped with matching red lipstick while blue eyeshadow lit up her bright blue eyes. Q whistled low. "My love, you look absolutely stunning."

Hilde ran her eyes up and down his body and returned the compliment. "You look rather handsome today as well. And happy."

"That's because I am," he said and placed a careful kiss on her painted lips.

Chapter 2

As they arrived at the Chinese restaurant near the famous shopping mall Kaufhaus des Westens, Hilde asked, "Do you think your friends suspect something?"

Q shrugged. "Let's go in and find out."

Erika and Gertrud were already waiting on them, together with Q's best friends, Jakob, Otto, and Leopold with his wife, Dörthe. They exchanged hugs with everyone, making the introductions and went to sit at the reserved table when Leopold eyed Hilde suspiciously. "So, what's the occasion for this get-together?"

Gertrud and Erika started giggling, and Hilde shot them an evil look. "Occasion?" She drawled out the word, squeezing Q's hand under the table.

Leopold cocked his head, looking from Hilde to Q and back. "You two are up to something. You look different."

Another fit of giggles came from the girls, and Jakob busied himself with the menu. All three of them had been sworn to secrecy.

"Different?" Hilde parroted his words and clasped her hand over her mouth to retain the violent giggle forming inside.

Dörthe's eyes went wide, and she shouted, "Look at the ring. She's wearing a ring!"

Q whispered into Hilde's ear, "Next time use the other hand," before he announced in a loud voice, "Hilde and I got married this morning."

Hilde managed to whisper back, "There won't be a next clandestine wedding for me," before everyone got up to congratulate them.

The waiter appeared as soon as everyone had settled down again and suggested they order the special five-course house menu for the eight of them. Everyone agreed, and he soon returned with a plum brandy on the house for the newlyweds and their guests.

The first course was Egg Drop Soup and the chatter at the table slowed down while eight hungry mouths dug into the delicious soup. Next, the waiter brought out a platter containing small egg rolls, lobster spring rolls, and pot stickers.

Hilde laughed out loud at the faces of her girlfriends searching for cutlery and pointed at the wooden chopsticks lying beside each plate. Erika sent her a startled glance. "You expect me to use…that?"

Q nodded and showed both Erika and Gertrud, who'd never eaten Chinese food before, how to use the chopsticks. The rest of the group merrily laughed at their clumsy efforts, and Hilde was glad she'd secretly perfected her domination of those treacherous sticks during the last week.

While Gertrud mastered the technique rather quickly, Erika gave up. The waiter apparently noticed her desperation and silently slid a fork beside her plate.

The dinner continued with lots of chatter and idle gossip by everyone, for once forgetting the difficult times. The main course consisted of sweet and sour chicken, fried rice, a spicy beef and vegetable dish, and teriyaki kabobs.

When the waiter finally removed their plates, Hilde leaned against Q. "There's no way I can eat even a single morsel of food more."

Q kissed her temple and smirked. "That's too bad for you. But I'll gladly eat your dessert."

"Eat my dessert? You better not! That might be grounds to ask for a divorce," she joked and giggled at his pouty face.

Q narrowed his eyes. "But you said you were full."

The waiter brought out a platter of desserts, fried bananas in honey, dumplings filled with poppy seeds and little pink, green, and white slimy balls Hilde couldn't identify. She licked her lips and armed herself with the chopsticks, saying, "If you didn't know it, I have one stomach for food and an entirely different one for dessert. And that one is still empty."

Everyone around the table laughed and deferred to the bride to take the first serving. Once both stomachs were full, her head whirled with the lively conversation, and she couldn't imagine a better way to end the day.

Jakob and Otto, though, could. They had discovered a new bar just a few short blocks away that served the most delicious Hungarian wines. The walk felt good. Hilde loved the way Q tenderly and possessively wrapped his arm around her shoulders. But even more, she loved the knowledge that from now on, they'd be going home together at the end of the night.

After more than one round of sweet Hungarian wine, Q leaned over to Leopold and reminded his friend of the first night he'd seen Hilde at the movie theater. "Told you she was going to be my wife."

Leopold sipped his wine. "Yes, you did. And I didn't believe it."

"You did what?" Hilde asked, but before she could say more, Erika produced a small package and gave it to the bridal couple.

Hilde opened the wrapping to reveal a book titled *1000 Spoonerisms and Shuffle Rhymes*.

After thanking Erika for the gift, Q took the book from Hilde's hand and said with a serious voice, "Let's see what we find in here." Then he opened the book on page twenty-four and recited the first verse:

Ich hoff', dass diese heile Welt

noch eine ganze Weile hält.

(I hope this perfect world

Will stay perfect for another while)

Hilde leaned against Q, tears of emotion filling her eyes. The outer world had stopped being perfect a long while ago, but her personal world had fallen into place like a puzzle. Admiring the ring on her finger, she thought, *Yes. It's a perfect world with Q, and I hope it'll last a lifetime.*

Then she opened the booklet on page twenty-seven, his birthday, and recited:

It is kisstomary to cuss the bride.

Everyone laughed as Q mockingly cursed her before taking her in his arms and kissing her. Hilde felt slightly tipsy, and she had no idea if it was the slaphappy atmosphere, the wine, or both.

Jacob took the book from her hand, and everyone took turns reciting verses, amidst much laughter and fun.

Do you see the butterfly, flutter by?

The Hungarian owners of the bar, as well as some of their countrymen, became curious about those hilarious Germans and joined them with more wine and their own funny rhymes until a dark-haired, bearded guy with the physique of a bull produced a guitar and started playing energetic melodies with passionate gypsy sounds.

After listening to the first song, Q asked the man if he could play the "Hungarian Dance No. 5" by Johannes Brahms for them. The man nodded. "Sure I can."

Q looked at Hilde with a mischievous grin.

"What?" she asked.

"I believe this is our traditional bridal waltz."

The man had started to play the captivating yet simple melody, and Q dragged Hilde to the makeshift dance floor beside the bar. "But this is not a waltz..." she protested faintly.

"And this wedding is not traditional," Q answered and captured her in his arms, leaving her no other recourse than to hold on for dear life and follow his steps. Soon everyone joined them, dancing, singing, and having fun.

Shortly before midnight, the group bid their new Hungarian friends goodbye, and the owner of the bar said, "I never thought Germans could be so funny. Keep this joy in your hearts, and your marriage will always prosper."

Back at home – their mutual home – they slipped into bed, tired after a long and exciting day. Q stroked her hair. "Did you have a good day?"

Hilde nodded. "The best. How about you?"

"Spectacular." He grew silent for a moment and then asked, "Are you terribly upset that we cannot embark on our honeymoon right away?"

She thought for a moment and then shook her head. "No. I like the idea of traipsing around Europe in the springtime much better than in the winter."

"Good. Oh, I forgot something." Q slipped from the bed and returned moments later with a leather-clad box in his hands. "This was delivered yesterday. It's from Carl and Emma."

Hilde sat up on the bed and took the box, opening it to reveal an elegant yet simple silver cutlery set. She trailed a finger over the smooth material that quickly warmed under her touch.

"It's not engraved..." he said.

She shook her head. "I wouldn't want it to be. My father would have known that. It's perfect."

"So are you."

Hilde returned the spoon to the leather box. "I love you, Dr. Wilhelm Quedlin. Thank you for this wonderful day."

Chapter 3

Q and Hilde paid a visit to his mother, recounting the happenings of their wedding day.

Ingrid greeted them with hot tea and home-baked gingerbread cookies. Her entire apartment smelled of cinnamon, ginger, and clove. It was early December, but in Q's opinion, it was never too early to eat Christmas cookies. He inhaled deeply, his mouth watering as he sat at the small kitchen table.

"When will you go on your honeymoon?" his mother asked.

Q glanced at Hilde in her simple midnight-blue turtleneck sweater and black pants. It was still a miracle to him that they were finally married. "Not before springtime. We want to travel across Europe for at least three months."

"Three months? That's a rather long time. How did you get that much vacation, Hilde?"

Q was a freelancer at the Biological Reich Institute and had both the possibility and the means to take extended time off, but Hilde was employed at an insurance company, processing claims.

Hilde's face lit up. "I've requested an unpaid leave of absence from my work, and the company agreed."

Because the Nazi ideology doesn't want married women working, Q thought bitterly.

For once, the Nazi ideology actually worked in their favor, which might be the part that angered him most. He'd come to hate the Nazis so much, he just couldn't enjoy Hilde's vacation the way she did.

His mother, perceptive as ever, took his hand and searched his eyes. "Darling, you should be thankful for this opportunity. Leaving Berlin for a bit will be a relief for you both, I would imagine."

A shiver ran down his spine, and he wondered how much his mother really knew or suspected of his subversive work.

"Yes, Mom, we're looking forward to it, aren't we?" Q said, reaching over and squeezing Hilde's hand.

She all but hopped up and down on her chair. "I'm so excited. We've planned a Grand Tour starting in Spain and then working our way back through France, Switzerland, and Italy. We'll get to see all those fantastic places like the Alhambra, Madrid, Barcelona, Paris, the Pyrenees, the Alps, and the Mediterranean of course..."

Ingrid smiled at the obvious enthusiasm Hilde showed. "You've had such a hard time getting married. Enjoy yourselves while you still can. Soon enough, you'll have the patter of little feet demanding your attention which will make trips like this much more difficult."

Children? Me? Prior to meeting Hilde, he'd never given it much thought, but now he imagined a sweet little girl with her blue eyes and the same enthusiasm. Sounds of laughter. The smell of baby.

Before they left, Ingrid gave each of them a wedding gift.

"Mom, you shouldn't have," Q protested, but his mother would hear nothing of it.

"Open it!"

Hilde unwrapped her small parcel and found a beautiful red jasper pendant with a golden necklace inside. Ingrid helped her to put it on and explained, "This is the lucky stone for your zodiac sign. And God knows we all are in need of some luck during these difficult times."

Then it was Q's turn to open his present. He found a letter opener adorned with a purple amethyst and grinned. He hated the way most people opened their letters. It left rugged edges. "Thank you so much, Mom. It's beautiful. And practical."

***

For a while, everything returned to normal. But preparing for an extended trip outside the country had proved to be almost as troublesome as obtaining their marriage license.

Once again, they made the trip to various offices and embassies to request passports, visas, and travel permissions. Q's previous trips to other European countries – including the last one four years ago to Paris, helping French warfare chemists – had been a piece of cake in comparison.

All those little obstacles showed Q just how much the Nazi's had already tightened their grip around Germany and her citizens, and how much the neighboring countries were in alarm. His mother was right; they should see the world while they still could, but the real threat to their freedom of travel was war, not children.

One day, Q attended one of the conspiratorial meetings with like-minded people who supported the idea of communism. It was disguised as a literature club, and he left the laboratory with *The Robbers* by Friedrich Schiller in his briefcase.

The walk to the Technical University of Berlin was short, and as always, they shut the doors tightly after everyone had arrived. Just today, *everyone* meant him, old Reinhard, and Johanna, a twenty-something blonde.

Q asked them, "Where's everyone else?"

Reinhard shook his head, but Johanna offered some information. "Kurt and Wilfried were arrested earlier this week."

"Arrested? What for?" Q asked, feeling the shock spread through his body.

Johanna scoffed. "For reading the wrong kind of books."

"You're kidding me," he said, but the sad shake of her head told him otherwise.

"The Gestapo found several books of Erich Maria Remarque and other banned authors in their possession and hauled them away. We haven't heard anything about their fates in three days."

Q swallowed a lump in his throat. Vivid images of bloody flesh and the rancid smell of mortal fear entered his mind. He shivered. "And the rest...?"

Reinhard answered, "It's not safe anymore to come here. We should stop meeting."

Johanna nodded.

"You can't just give up. Not now, when we're needed the most. It's no longer just about helping Russia, it's about tearing Germany from the clutches of evil and destruction." Q ran a hand through his curls, pacing up and down the small study room in the University building.

"It's just the three of us. The others have already decided not to come anymore." It was the knowing voice of someone who'd seen unimaginable terrors in the Great War that made Q realize the extent of the decision being discussed. "I'm nearing eighty," Reinhard continued, "and Johanna is just a young girl. And you – you're recently married. We're not the material heroes are made of."

"You're serious..." Q whispered.

Johanna cast her eyes to the ground, unable to meet Q's. "I'm sorry. It's just...I want to live." Then she picked up her volume of *The Robbers* and left.

Q looked into the knowing eyes of Reinhard, who took his cane and prepared to leave as well. Before he reached the door, he turned once more to stare at Q and said, "I'm not of much use for our cause anymore, but you my son, you go ahead and do what you must."

When the door closed behind the old man, Q closed his eyes to keep tears from falling. Suddenly, he felt desolate.

The last man standing.

Chapter 4

Late in April 1937, Hilde and Q finally finished their preparations and were set to travel when another escalation in the Spanish Civil War – the bombing of Guernica – caused them to change their plans at the last minute. Q even asked his Russian contact about the situation. The agent had enough background information to advise strongly against visiting Spain or France at that time.

Hilde looked out the window as the train pulled into the station at Breuil-Cervinia ski resort in northwestern Italy, her eyes going wide at the sight of the majestic mountains rising up from the valley floor. Lush greens at the bottom gave way to rugged grey escarpment topped by white dollops of whipped cream.

During the long hours of their two-day journey, she amused herself by looking out the window and cataloging the things she saw. Breathtaking scenery with rolling hills, dark forests, and small villages. Fields of daffodils and roadside poppies announcing spring. Quaint little lake and fields that looked so perfect, it was hard to place them as existing only a few hundred miles from Berlin where dread and terror lurked behind every corner.

Far away from the capital, the only shadows obscuring her light-hearted mind had been the occasional stops along the way where police officers would board the train to ask the passengers for a brief inspection of paperwork.

Each time Q handed over their papers, she involuntarily held her breath, not relaxing until the officer handed them back and left their compartment.

As they crossed the Swiss border, Hilde finally relaxed. But now, after being cooped up inside the train for so many hours, she longed to breathe fresh air once again.

The train stopped.

"We're here!" Hilde exclaimed and grabbed her bag to jump off the train in a hurry.

"I can see that," Q answered with a grin. He slowed her down by placing a hand upon her lower back and together they made their way off the train.

Q collected their suitcases from the luggage wagon and then gestured for her to join him as they went in search of their hotel. The valley floor was showing signs of spring, but despite the blinding sun, the air carried a definite chill.

"Look, the mountains are still covered with snow," she said with a glance at the breathtaking scenery surrounding them. "Doesn't it look exactly like the pictures we've seen?"

"That's good, isn't it?" he asked good-naturedly.

Hilde laughed and skipped ahead a bit. "I want to go skiing."

"Skiing will have to wait until tomorrow. It's way past lunchtime already."

"Oh," she said with a pout, but then brightened, determined to only see the bright side of things. "That's okay, we'll be much more rested tomorrow."

They arrived at the hotel, and while not a grand structure, it impressed with sand colored stone walls that had weathered over the centuries and flower boxes at the windows filled with blossoming geraniums in orange and red hues.

"Isn't that lovely?" Hilde exclaimed as they entered the cozy building and the receptionist led them upstairs to their room.

"I hope this room will be okay?" the young man inquired as he opened the door to let them inside.

Q nodded. "I'm sure it will be fine." But Hilde rushed inside and plopped onto the queen sized bed, stretching out her limbs. "I love the place."

Their host nodded and helped Q carry in the rest of their luggage before bowing his head and leaving them to explore the room by themselves. Hilde stood again, wandered over to the closest window and pushed the curtains wide, gasping at the sight before her.

"Q, you have to see this, the Matterhorn is right over there," she said, pointing to the large mountain peak framed by the wooden window. While Breuil-Cervinia lay in Italy, the impressive mountain range in the Northeast belonged to Switzerland.

He joined her at the window to appreciate the panorama, giving her a smile before returning to unpack their belongings.

Hilde let her eyes wander over the small village spread out below her, and a sense of excitement and adventure made her giggle like a schoolgirl.

"What's so funny?" Q asked, setting a pair of shoes just inside the armoire tucked in the corner of the room.

"I can't believe we're finally here," Hilde answered, spreading her arms wide and spinning in a small circle.

Q grinned at her, catching her around the waist and dancing her across the room. "Believe it."

She nodded, dizzy with joy and spinning in circles. This was paradise. Unpacking could wait, she had to explore first and walked towards the other window of their corner room. The mountain chain that spread out before her now wasn't nearly as magnificent, but Hilde had read in the travel guide that the highest peaks were nearly eleven thousand feet above sea level and were covered with glacier ice year round.

Great fissures and treacherous slopes awaited those foolish enough to climb outside of the groomed areas, but she didn't feel afraid to venture up the mountain. Instead, she felt a sense of freedom she hadn't experienced since knowing about Q's subversive intelligence activities.

In Berlin, she lived with a constant fear that he would be found out. Every time she spied an SS or Gestapo officer on the streets, she felt a chill run down her spine, always terrified she'd hear the dreaded words, "Stop. You're traitors working against the Führer and Fatherland."

More than once, she'd stopped breathing until they had walked on by, just to come up breathless with a red face. *What a way to act unsuspicious.* Those moments had become a common occurrence, and it wasn't until now that she realized how tense her life had become.

She hadn't heard Q's steps and started when he laid a hand on her shoulder. "Love, you can watch that panorama all you want in the next days, but I'm starving. Why don't you unpack, and we'll go in search of dinner? Our host suggested a little Italian place in the village that serves excellent pasta."

Did he? When? Hilde turned in Q's arms and kissed him. "Hmm. Pasta sounds perfect. I'm hungry, too." She made short work of emptying her suitcase. She set her shoes alongside Q's, hung up her dresses, skirts, blouses, and slacks, and used the top drawer of the bureau with the large oval mirror attached to stash her unmentionables.

"Ready," she said a few minutes later.

Q nodded approvingly and placed both of their suitcases beneath the bed. "We won't be needing these for a while." He headed for the door, grabbing his coat and hat, suggesting she do the same. "It will be cold once the sun goes down."

Hilde had already grabbed her coat and added a hat and a pair of gloves as well. "I'm already having fun."

Q led her down the staircase, then stopped to speak with their host for a moment to ask for directions to the recommended restaurant. Ten minutes later, they were stepping inside the small establishment, smiles on their faces as they were greeted with enthusiasm.

A well-fed man directed them to a table for two. *"Benvenuti Signori!"*

Q helped Hilde take off her coat and handed it to the man. The menu though was a surprise. Written exclusively in Italian, they had difficulties choosing what to eat. Instead of deciphering the meaning of words like *salsiccia, pisello,* or *melanzana,* they decided to put their choice into the hands of the waiter and upon his return, Q asked him to surprise two ravenous travelers with the best food he had.

Hilde laughed as the corpulent man clapped his hands and bustled away. "He seems happy with your decision."

Before Q could reply, the waiter returned with an opened bottle of red wine. He poured them both a glass and said in his broken German, "Wine of the house."

Hilde admired the deep red tone of the liquid and raised the glass to sniff the wine. A rich, flowery yet sweet scent wafted to her nostrils, and she smiled in appreciation. When she took a sip, the rich, tangy flavor burst upon her tongue, leaving a trace of nut as she swallowed.

"Excellent wine," she murmured, taking another sip.

"Definitely," Q responded. "I guess the Italian wine is famous for a reason."

The *primo piatto,* first course, arrived, and Hilde stared at the delicacies brought to them. Noodles covered in a seasoned tomato sauce, meatballs that exploded with flavor, and slices of homemade bread with melted butter dripping from them.

Hilde was almost full when the waiter arrived with their *secondo piatto,* the main dish, with the most tender meat and crisp, steamed vegetables. And just when she thought her belly would burst, the waiter returned with more food: ice-cream and then cheese.

As they finished their meal, she slipped onto the bench beside Q and leaned against him, sipping her wine and listening as the locals celebrated...what, she didn't know, but it was obvious there was a celebration of some sort going on. Toasts were made. Songs were sung. Couples laughed together, and as the evening wore on, she felt so very blessed to be sharing this moment with Q.

It was the happiest she'd been since the moment she said, "Yes, I do" in front of the magistrate many months ago. For once, she didn't have to look over her shoulder or be careful what she said.

She was blissfully happy in this moment, and as her eyes met Q's and he caressed her arm, his eyes echoed her sentiment. Pure happiness.

Chapter 5

The next morning, Q awoke with the sun tickling his eyes as it crept through their window. For a moment, he had no idea where he was. He'd slept so peacefully and better than he had in a long time. *Italy.* He blinked against the sunlight and rolled over to kiss Hilde awake. Her soft shoulders smelled of wine and roses. He inhaled her unique scent, remembering the evening before. "Good morning, sleeping beauty, ready to go skiing?"

Her eyes fluttered open, and a bright smile lit her face when she nodded. "Yes."

"Good. Let's get dressed and have breakfast downstairs before we embark upon our adventure."

Q kissed her forehead, and they both hurried through their morning ablutions, dressing warmly for their excursion up the mountain, excited about the day ahead.

They settled in the hotel's breakfast room, and while eating, Q asked the receptionist for directions. First, they headed towards a small shop to rent ski equipment. Despite the language barrier, they got everything they needed and soon enough took the gondola up to the top of the mountain, from where they planned to ski back down to the village.

From the valley floor, it seemed like an excellent plan, and neither Q nor Hilde gave a thought to how difficult skiing down from the top might be.

The gondola ride up the mountain was magical, and Q watched in amusement as Hilde tried to see everything at once. Her gaze kept straying to the massive mountains that rose up in the distance.

"It's so beautiful," she repeated over and over. If she'd loved watching nature on their train journey, then she was now utterly enthralled by the majestic mountain panorama. Far away, the Matterhorn rose above the other peaks, but the much lower and closer mountains on the Italian side weren't any less impressive.

Q closed his eyes for a moment and felt the stress they'd been living under slowly fade away. He knew when they returned to Berlin, it would come rushing back quicker than they would have preferred, but for these next weeks and months, he didn't want to think about threats and danger.

Meanwhile, the gondola had reached the top and slowed to a crawl. An attendant, dressed warmly in hat, coat, and mittens, assisted them off the lift car with their skiing equipment. Q shivered as they made their way out to the open slope. It was fairly flat near the gondola station, and he and Hilde took their time putting on their skis, making sure everything was buckled up correctly.

Donning his cap and watching as she did the same, he asked, "Ready?" A sign at the top had indicated several paths to choose from, but not understanding fully what the symbols and colors meant, he elected to ignore it and followed the route most of the other skiers were taking.

Hilde nodded, and he pushed off, gliding along the pleasantly graded slope with a feeling of relief and freedom. But his smile quickly gave way to concern and then a shadow of foreboding as the slope narrowed and steepened drastically. *What did that sign mean? I should have asked someone.*

He managed to keep himself upright, zigzagging back and forth across the steep hill, glancing back every few seconds to make sure Hilde was managing to do the same. He'd not even made it a third of the way down when her anguished cry reached him.

Q dug the side of his skis into the snow and came to a stop, using his poles to keep his balance while he looked up to see Hilde lying in the snow, her legs tangled, one ski lying several feet away from her.

"Darling, are you hurt?" he shouted up to her, swallowing down the rising panic as he released his own skis and made his way up to her.

"I fell," she whimpered.

"I can see that. Are you injured?"

Hilde tried to get up. "My knee…it hurts."

Q squatted down next to her and removed her other ski, helping her sit up. Then he gently probed around her knee, observing how she scrunched her nose with discomfort. He shook his head. "You can't ski down in this condition. We'll walk back up to the lift and ride it down."

"No!" she said, shaking her head vehemently. "I didn't come all this way to ride in the gondola. I want to ski down."

"I don't think it's wise to risk further injury to your knee…" Q sighed. Her face had taken on that mulish look he'd come to know so well. Her mind was made up, and there was nothing in the world that would convince her otherwise.

"I'll take my time and be more cautious. I can do this." She gave him a watery smile, putting on her brave face. In response, all he could do was nod.

"Are you sure? This hill is much steeper than it looked at the beginning. What if it gets harder?"

"I'm going to enjoy myself," she answered, using her poles to push herself to a standing position. "Could you bring me the other ski, please?"

Against his better judgment, Q retrieved her other ski and held her arm for balance as he secured it to her foot. "Are you sure you don't want to walk back to the gondola?" He tried one last time to convince her. The village was a long way down from here.

"I'm sure." She tested her weight on the injured knee, and to her credit, he didn't even see her flinch. "See, I'm fine. How about I go first since I'll probably be slower than you?"

Q nodded and made his way back down to where he'd left his skis. Putting them on, he then followed behind Hilde, his eyes never wavering from her as she attempted to stay upright. They reached the bottom of the first hill, and Q skied up next to her. "How are you doing?"

Hilde tried to smile, but it didn't reach her eyes. "This is much harder than I remembered."

"I could try…"

She pursed her lips. "No, let's keep going."

Q watched her push off again. If he weren't so worried, he'd be proud of her. Hilde fought her way down the slope, unyielding in her determination to master it. But she fell repeatedly, and by the time they reached then next small landing, she was breathing heavily and having trouble regaining her feet again.

The sun had reached its zenith and mercilessly burnt down on them. Q felt the sting of its rays on his pale winter skin. At least it was warm. When he spotted a flat patch, he convinced Hilde to sit down and take a rest. They ate and drank their meager provisions, and while the mountain range lay still and peaceful as before, Q now felt an overwhelming respect for the power it represented.

Coming from the flats of Northern Germany, they'd both severely underestimated the hazards of the mountain area. At the moment, he worried about the unforgiving rays of the sun, but that would soon change.

"Hilde, darling…"

"Q, don't look so worried," she said, looking refreshed after their break. He traced his fingers down her red cheeks, and she winced at the touch. "You're getting burned."

Hilde gave a rueful laugh. "That's amazing since I'm freezing. My feet are so cold, I can barely feel my toes."

"We need to keep moving, Hilde. Can you make it?"

***

Yes, she could. She had to – it was the only way out. Hilde cursed her own stupidity and murmured under her breath, "I should have listened to you. This is much too difficult for a beginner like me."

She fell again into the harsh white snow. Getting up proved more difficult each time, and by now, not only was her knee screaming with pain, but her entire body wanted her to stop moving.

Earlier, the sun had burnt her tender face, but now as they skied into the shadow of the peaks towering over them, and the cold breeze kicked up, her teeth were chattering and her fingers barely able to clutch her poles.

The biting cold wind whipped right through her woolen sweater and the layers beneath. With the number of times Hilde had fallen, her clothing had become encrusted with snow and was now soaking. The icy moisture seeped through her other layers, and with every move, the wet cotton disgustingly clung to her body, intensifying the bone chills.

I'm a fool. I wanted to prove I could do this, but why?

Q cheered her on and encouraged her to get up after each fall, but he couldn't fool her. His eyes indicated he was worried beyond measure.

"I'm sorry, I should have listened to you," she said the next time he helped her up.

"Don't worry, my love, we'll make it," Q said as they rounded the top of the next hill and gestured at the village lying directly ahead of them, separated only by a broad and flat hill. From there it was only a few minutes walk to their hotel, but Hilde was so exhausted, she could barely remain upright, let alone carry her own skis.

He noticed before she could say a word and carried both sets of skis, using his free arm to steady her as she limped along beside him. Q left the skis outside the front lobby and then Hilde closed her eyes as he scooped her up in his arms and carried her up the stairs to their room.

What had started out as a wonderfully exciting day had turned into a skiing nightmare. She collapsed onto the bed, sinking onto the edge of the mattress, near to tears with relief. Her body demanded sleep.

"Hilde! Wake up!"

Why didn't he let her sleep? "I'm so tired."

Q's voice reached her through the fog of exhaustion, but she couldn't make much sense of it. "You need to get out of your wet clothing and then I'll have a look at your knee."

Whatever it was he wanted to do to her, she didn't care. Like a puppet on a string, she rolled from side to side, lifted her legs and arms whenever he requested it, all with the intention to make him go away and let her sleep.

"Hildelein, darling, you're shivering."

Strange. She wasn't cold. In fact, she didn't *feel* anything. Not even the sheets beneath her or his hands on her body as he pushed the flannel nightgown down her torso.

"Into bed with you now," Q urged her, plumping up the pillows behind her back and tucking the quilt around her shoulders. "I'll see if I can round up some hot tea for you. Stay in bed and get warm."

"Q?" she called after him when he started to leave the room.

"Yes?" he turned, giving her a quizzical look.

"I'm tired."

"I know, darling. Sleep, I'll be right back." Giving in to her exhaustion, her eyes must have fluttered shut, because she didn't see him leave the room, nor did she notice his return bearing a tray with hot water, cups, sugar, cream, and tea. He woke her, holding a cup of steaming tea to her lips, forcing her to take careful sips.

The hot liquid ran down her throat, and for a short moment, everything got worse. She became painfully aware of the congelation in her limbs, and as her feet and hands thawed, pins and needles tortured her. Her hands shivered so badly, Q took the cup from her and held it himself, feeding her more tiny sips of heat.

Delicious heat.

With the warmth, life returned to her limbs and her brain. "I'm sorry for ruining our first honeymoon day."

"Don't be sorry, my love. I'm just glad we made it back to the hotel. I called a doctor for you."

"I don't need a doctor. I just need to rest..." But the distressed look in his bright blue eyes made her stop midsentence. If Q needed her to be seen by a doctor to stop worrying, so be it.

"I want a doctor to look at your knee and your sunburn, just to make sure," he said, stroking her hair. "You're still shivering."

"I don't know if I'll ever feel warm again," she murmured and slumped back into the pillows.

"Drink some more tea, then I'll see about finding you another blanket."

Hilde dutifully drank the hot liquid he held to her lips, each sip bringing back sensation to her body. When he prepared to leave to fetch another blanket, she found the strength to reach for his arm. "Don't leave again."

"You're still cold."

"Snuggle with me. That would warm me up." Hilde tried a small smile, and he gave in to her request, slipped off his shoes, and climbed onto the other side of the bed to gather her in his arms, tucking the quilt around her body like a cocoon.

Hilde dozed off in the security that the man she loved watched over her until a brisk knocking on the door announced the arrival of the doctor. Q invited him in and then paced at the end of the bed while the doctor examined her injured knee.

"Signora Quedlin, it appears you've pulled a tendon and strained the muscles from your knee down your calf and across the top of your foot. How did you say this injury occurred?"

"Well, I fell when we attempted to ski down from the top of the mountain…"

"What? Are you experienced skiers?" the doctor inquired, looking between Q and Hilde.

She shook her head. "I've been once before…"

The doctor muttered something in Italian that sounded like a curse word and looked angry. "You tourists are so irresponsible at times. These mountains are not for beginners. Did you not see the warning sign at the top?"

Q nodded. "I did, but I have to confess the colors and symbols didn't mean anything to me."

"You're lucky one of you wasn't seriously injured. Next time, stay on the blue slopes close to the village."

"We will," Q answered, feeling the sting of the chastisement.

"Good," the doctor replied, seeming somewhat mollified by Q's response. "Your wife will need to rest her knee for several days before she can try skiing again." He packed up his supplies and Q escorted him to the door.

Hilde's eyelids closed and she was already half asleep when she heard Q's voice, "Are you hungry?"

"No. Just tired."

"Then sleep." A kiss on her nose was the last thing she felt before the land of dreams claimed her.

***

She woke the next morning and attempted to roll over in the bed, only to gasp as a sharp pain rushed from her ankle to her knee. "Ouch!"

"Hilde?" Q's voice came from the other side of the room. He was already up and fully dressed.

"My knee hurts." She carefully sat up and stared at the swollen joint. It was easily double the size of the other knee, and the skin featured all colors of the rainbow, from a light yellow, to greens and blues, to dark black bruises on the bones.

"You're a piece of art," Q said, following her gaze and obviously thinking the same. "And the red colors are up here." He gestured at her sunburnt face. "Let me get some lotion."

The cool liquid he rubbed into her face soothed the tight stinging sensation on her cheekbones, and she sighed. "Much better."

"Yes, we both got a little too much sun yesterday. I already bought sunscreen."

Hilde looked at Q's bright red face and reached for the lotion to rub the cool liquid on his stubbly face.

A loud growl came from her stomach, and she pushed herself to a sitting position before asking, "Could you help me get dressed?"

"Why?"

She pressed her hand to her rumbling belly. "I'm hungry. We should go to breakfast."

Q grinned. "Well, breakfast sounds like a wonderful idea. Can you manage the stairs, or should I throw you over my shoulder like a flour sack?"

Hilde slapped his shoulder. "Don't you dare!"

He grinned some more, assisted her in getting dressed, then helped her downstairs to the breakfast room.

They spent several lazy days talking with other travelers and getting a feel for the small village's amenities, soaking in the wild and rugged yet peaceful atmosphere of the Alps. Nothing here resembled the frightful life in Berlin and Hilde couldn't remember a time in her life she'd enjoyed more, even hampered as she was by her injury.

The threats in Breuil-Cervinia didn't come from humans, but from nature. Like the frequent snow slides crashing down the scarps on the other side of the valley, their thunderous noise often tore up the silence in the village, echoing manifold back and forth between the mountain walls.

But in contrast to the hidden yet omnipresent danger in their hometown, it was much easier to avoid the threats of nature.

A week later, they attempted to ski again, with much more success this time. They stuck to the blue beginner's slopes, and after a day or two, neither of them were even falling all that much.

Their honeymoon in Italy was turning out to be perfect. No problems. No worries. No watching what one said and to whom they were talking. Freedom. Something neither of them – especially Q – had experienced in so many years.

Chapter 6

As June arrived, so did their time to leave the Alps.
They boarded the train, bound for Sicily, and Q was
more in love now than ever before.

They finally arrived in Naples just as the sun was
rising above the horizon, and even though they'd only
gotten a few hours of sleep, they were more than ready
to play tourist once again.

Hilde had disappeared behind the retractable
changing screen to put on one of the summer dresses
she'd bought for the trip. When she didn't come out
again, Q asked anxiously, "Are you ready to explore
the city?"

"Almost," she answered, and Q continued to gather
their things. The train had already slowed to a crawl as
it moved through the outskirts of the city, passing
historic ruins of times gone by.

But as Hilde stepped out from behind the screen, he
all but dropped the things in his hands, whistling low
and long as he stared at her. She looked stunning in her
lightweight dress in an A-line cut with flared skirts,
puffed sleeves, and a gathered bodice that rested just

below her bustline. The bright colors flattered her and brought out the glimmer in her blue eyes.

He ran his fingers down the patterned fabric of the dress that was perfect for a warm summer day. "Hilde, you are gorgeous. By far the most beautiful woman in all of Italy. No, in all of Europe."

Hilde blushed and giggled. "Thank you."

"I shall have to beat the men off with a stick," Q murmured as they exited the train. They'd stay in the port city a few days until they'd secured a ferry to Palermo on the island of Sicily.

Naples was a mixture of history, some of it dating back over several thousand years. Castles, churches, and testaments to the great Roman Empire, and in the distance, the imposing silhouette of Mount Vesuvius towered like a silent guardian.

"Can you see it?" Hilde asked him as they explored the center of the city.

"See what?" he asked, letting his gaze wander around.

"What it must have been like to live during the time of the Romans? I can almost hear the chariots coming down the street." She inhaled deeply.

Q grinned and imitated her, smelling the scent of oranges and jasmine strong in the air. "And I can smell rotten fish, human waste, and the remains of victims of the plague."

"You're so...so...unromantic," she sputtered.

"You're right. I'm sorry," he answered and gathered her in his arms.

"Wouldn't it be nice to actually *experience* how life was back then?" Hilde asked.

Q thought for a moment and frowned. "I should invent a time machine so you can go back and become a Roman lady." He laughed at the hopeful gleam in her eyes. Tweaking her nose, he chuckled, "I'm not sure that's even possible, so allow your fertile imagination to run wild."

Hilde giggled. "My imagination will work just fine. Besides, I'm not at all sure you'd look good in a tunic."

He raised a brow at her and then shook his head. "I'm sure I would not enjoy being dressed like that. My knees are knobby."

She giggled some more, happy and carefree. As they wandered farther into the city, Hilde was shocked by the conditions she and Q encountered. The amount of poverty displayed was appalling. Kids and adults alike dressed in nothing but tattered and dirty rags. Shanty houses with only one room served as living, cooking, and sleeping quarters for the entire family. Most of the homes had no doors, merely rags or sheets partially covering the doorframes.

"Q, how can these people live like this?" she asked in a whispered voice that no one but he could hear.

He shook his head. "I truly don't know. Things are bad in Germany, but not this bad. I didn't believe I would ever say this, but the living conditions in Germany are much better than here."

And they were, but then he noticed something else. Even though the people of Naples were poverty stricken, most of them had friendly smiles on their faces. He commented on this to Hilde. "Look at their faces."

Hilde did and scrunched her nose in thought. "They're happy. Much happier than the people in Berlin."

***

A few days later, they took the ferry to Palermo, which was as noisy, dirty, and poor as Naples. They quickly embarked on the next train along the coast until they got off in a lovely seaside village to find a place to stay.

It was already early evening when they found the perfect small hotel with hot spas supplied with boiling water from a nearby inactive volcano. They were both tired and hungry. Q tipped the man at the reception desk to help cart their luggage to their room, then he arranged for a light meal to be brought to them by the host of the small restaurant next to the hotel, who was more than happy to earn a few extra bills for his effort.

Hilde made use of the washroom to rinse the dirt of the trip from her feet, and then she washed her exposed arms, neck, and face. She was just blotting the excess moisture from her skin when Q stepped into the small space, having the same idea.

"I can't believe how crowded and dirty Palermo was," she said.

"Yes, it was even worse than Naples, but this village is cute and clean," he answered as he washed his hands and arms.

Q finished rinsing his face and then the receptionist arrived with the dinner he'd requested. They ate in relative silence, letting the happenings of the past days replay in their minds.

Later Hilde was gazing out the window when he sat down next to her, pulling her into the crook of his arm.

"Have I told you today how much I adore you?" He placed a kiss on her hair, just above her ear.

Hilde turned and met his gaze. "No."

"Well, I do. You're the best thing that has ever happened to me in my entire life. If I had to die now, I'd die content and with a smile on my face, because I'd known you and loved you."

She kissed him. "You're not to talk about dying, at least not anytime soon. We don't have to be afraid here. This is our blissful time to just enjoy being together. Without a care in the world."

Q nodded. "That is true. For the first time in years, I'm not constantly looking over my shoulder. I'm so thankful for our time here together."

"I too am thankful. I know Naples wasn't what we expected, but I cannot help contrasting the differences between the citizens of Naples and those of Berlin. These people have so little, and yet they can find a reason to smile and laugh. In Germany, people are afraid to laugh."

"Let's not talk about home. Let's get some sleep," he said and undressed to go to bed.

The tiny village and the hotel turned out to be a small paradise, and they met many foreign tourists from Russia, Sweden, England, France, and several other places. Just the day before, an English couple had joined their table at a small café and upon learning that he and Hilde hailed from Germany, a discussion concerning the Nazis had ensued. Q had been sitting on needles afraid Hilde might say too much and give away their secret. It was one thing to admit that they weren't very fond of the Nazis, but an entirely different one to be actively involved in the resistance.

They were sitting in the lounge of the hotel drinking an afternoon coffee when Q cautioned Hilde, "Even though most people here are friendly and probably share our opinion, we can't let them know about...you know."

"I would never commit that mistake," Hilde assured him, lowering her voice. "Even though Germany is many miles away from here, the Nazis have eyes and ears all over." And they did. The Nazis had an extensive reach across Europe.

She continued to talk about something, but Q had stopped listening and groaned.

"What's wrong?" she asked, concerned.

He gestured briefly towards the other side of the lobby. "You'll never believe who just arrived here."

Chapter 7

Hilde followed Q's gaze and gasped.

The well-built man with the military cut grey hair and the piercing green eyes looked a lot younger than his almost sixty years. His impressive presence filled the lobby, and all chatter had died down to a whisper upon his arrival.

He wore the dress uniform of the Deutsche Wehrmacht, the German Army, and though neither Hilde nor Q had met him before, she instantly recognized the handsome man as Generalfeldmarschall Werner von Blomberg, Commander-in-Chief of the Armed Forces and Minister of War.

A chill rushed down her spine. She'd felt so safe in Italy and now this.

"Q?"

Q shook his head, indicating this was not the time for her questions. Despite his nonchalant behavior, she could feel the anxiety radiating off of him, and a dull suspicion crossed her mind. He'd behaved oddly all day, and he'd insisted they take their coffee in the lounge and wait...for...the Minister of War?

Hilde's chest constricted. *No, that's not possible. Or is it?*

"What haven't you told me, Wilhelm Quedlin?" she asked him in a stern whisper.

Q squirmed under her stare. "I thought von Blomberg was a widower. So who's the woman clinging to his arm?"

Woman? Glancing back, Hilde noticed the curvaceous brunette standing beside von Blomberg and casting loving glances at him. "That woman can't be older than twenty-five; she must be his daughter."

"Looking at him like a love-sick puppy? Not likely." Q smirked.

"Are you going to answer my question?" Hilde pressed him.

Q sighed. "I'm supposed to be meeting with a Russian agent assigned to Italy."

Hilde's eyes opened wide. "Why didn't you tell me?"

"I just did."

She leaned closer. "That wasn't what I meant."

"I know. I was hoping to avoid this altogether." A flurry of activity was now taking place in the foyer of the hotel as every available employee rushed to make the Generalfeldmarschall and his guest comfortable.

Q was sitting sideways at the table, and Hilde watched him as he continued to drink his coffee, his face shuttered and without expression. That is, until von Blomberg took notice of them and approached their table.

He greeted them with a "Heil Hitler" and Hilde watched the brief moment of disgust flash in Q's eyes. Meeting her gaze briefly, he stood to his feet and returned the greeting, raising his hand and offering a *Hitlergruss* to von Blomberg.

Hilde took her cue from Q and followed suit, not wanting to draw undue attention to them.

"I can recognize a good Aryan when I see him. Where are you from?" von Blomberg explained and waved an employee over to bring two more chairs and coffee. Without asking, he and his companion sat at Q's and Hilde's table.

Hilde's throat was dry as the desert at noon, and for the life of her, she couldn't say a word. With her heart thundering in her throat, she grabbed onto Q's hand like a lifeline.

Thankfully, Q was more composed and dutifully answered von Blomberg's question. "My wife and I are from Berlin. It's an honor to meet you, Herr Generalfeldmarschall."

"None of those formalities. Luise and I are here exclusively on personal business," he said with a doting look at the young woman.

While he and Q exchanged pleasantries, Hilde gave the younger woman a tight smile. "I'm Hilde. Pleased to meet you."

Luise obviously came from a humble background and felt slightly uncomfortable in the limelight. Hilde's heart warmed, and she pitied the girl – almost.

"It's so nice meeting some other people from Germany here. I hope you don't mind us joining you? The travel was tiring."

Isn't it a bit late to ask? Now that you're already sitting at our table? But Hilde bit down her remark, and as she couldn't think of a way to politely refuse, she nodded. "Not at all."

Coffee arrived and with each sip of the aromatic liquid, Luise came out of her shell and chatted away. Hilde wanted to jump up and rush from the room. Instead, she patiently conversed about the weather, dresses, and all of the exciting things they'd seen and done while on their travels.

She glanced over to Q for help, but he wasn't in any better situation than she was.

***

Q surreptitiously glanced at the clock hanging on the wall, worried his Russian contact was going to show up at any minute and run straight into the Generalfeldmarschall.

Von Blomberg updated him on the glorious Nazis progress in several areas, and Q did his best to pretend interest and joy. Apparently with success, because von Blomberg leaned back in his chair and pierced Q with his alert green eyes. "You're a man after my liking. What's your contribution to the *Reich*?"

Q swallowed hard. *Do everything in my might to shorten its lifespan.* "I'm a chemical engineer, working for the Biological Reich Institute."

"A scientist." Von Blomberg seemed delighted and asked more questions about the kind of work Q was involved in.

Q put up a brave front and answered all his questions, while anxiety corroded his insides. He turned his head to Hilde, but she was deep in conversation with Luise. From her side, he couldn't hope for a rescue.

"We could use someone with your talents in the Wehrmacht," von Blomberg said, and Q almost doubled over. *He can't be serious, can he?*

"Sir, I'm afraid I'm much too old to be of any worth as a soldier," he protested faintly and then paled. A man who could only be the Russian agent had arrived and was heading straight for him, oblivious to the man sitting at his table.

Q shook his head violently, not so much as an answer to the Generalfeldmarschall, but with the intent to scare the agent away.

Von Blomberg laughed heartily. "Not as a soldier. The Ministry of War has a lot to offer a good scientist. In fact, we are in need of someone with your brilliant mind to head our research department. We're always working to find better and more efficient weapons."

To kill more people. I would rather kill myself than work for you.

The Russian approached closer, a searching look in his eyes. *He can't recognize von Blomberg because he sees only his back. If he says one wrong word, we're all in deep trouble.* Q could only hope the agent was experienced enough not to give them away with a silly action.

"...I believe you would do a credible job in that position," Von Blomberg continued, and Q felt as if someone tightened a rope around his neck. Beads of sweat formed on his forehead and worked their way down his temples. The agent was now mere yards from them.

Q wiped the sweat from his face with a kerchief and said louder than necessary, "I'm sorry. It's hot in here, Herr Generalfeldmarschall von Blomberg."

The man approaching him hesitated almost imperceptibly and made a beeline for the stairs leading to the floors with the guest rooms.

"None of those formalities. Please call me Werner," Von Blomberg said with a jovial grin. "We have a lot to discuss."

"Thank you, Herr…Werner. My name is Wilhelm," Q answered shakily. "That is a very generous offer, and I will certainly take it into consideration."

Out of the corner of his eye, he saw a hotel employee chasing behind the Russian who'd disappeared upstairs. Afraid of the tumult that might ensue and clue in von Blomberg about who the Russian was and why he was here, Q decided it was best to keep Werner's attention on what was happening at their table.

"Right now, I'm enjoying my honeymoon with my wife." He reached across the table and squeezed Hilde's thigh, causing her to blush prettily.

Werner glanced at her and laughed. "Young love. Isn't it adorable? But I must insist. We need men of your talent. Enjoy your honeymoon, and once you return to Berlin, report to my office."

Q started to respond, but the hotel director who'd been summoned from his office came to his rescue, greeting the Generalfeldmarschall and his companion, "Welcome to our hotel, sir, it's an honor to have you staying with us. I've personally seen that our best suite is prepared for you, if you'll follow me, please?"

Werner stood up and held a hand out to Luise before addressing Q, "I expect to converse some more with you during our stay here." He nodded at Hilde and walked off with the hotel director leading the way.

With a deep sigh, Q ushered Hilde towards the exit and out onto the sidewalk. His pulse drummed as if he'd been running a sprint and Hilde seemed to feel the same anxiety. He could smell the fear rolling off of her in waves.

In silence, they walked hand in hand until they ended on the nearby beach. Hilde stopped to remove her shoes and stockings to dip her feet into the cool water as it flowed back and forth across the packed sand.

The sound of the waves lapping on the beach had a calming effect, and he followed suit. Taking his shoes off, he tied their laces together and slung them around his neck, taking Hilde's hand in his own as they walked in silence.

He had to think. Ponder the consequences of meeting Werner von Blomberg. The reality of his dangerous life in Berlin had come crashing into the blissful enjoyment of the last few weeks. No matter how much he wished it were not so, they were never going to be completely safe.

Not in this world. Not as long as the Nazis were in power. Not even on their honeymoon.

Chapter 8

Hilde could tell that the events of the last hour had shaken Q to the core. Despite his calm exterior, it took only one look into his eyes to recognize the turmoil boiling inside him.

Without speaking a single word, they walked along the beach, his pace increasing until she could barely keep up with him. Hilde slipped her hand out of his and stopped, unsure if he'd even noticed because he kept on walking. A smile flickered on her lips. He'd come back when he was done thinking.

She sat down on the beach and patiently waited for his return while looking out at the horizon. Fleecy clouds floated across the deep blue sky, bringing a pattern of light and shadow to the ocean. Doubts and fears overshadowed the joy in her heart, dimming what should have been another wonderful day on the beach in the Mediterranean.

Q returned half an hour later, took her hand, and pulled her up against his chest. They held tight onto each other for a minute and even before he voiced the first word, she sensed his inner struggle.

"That was close. Too close." Q's voice could barely be heard above the waves.

"It was close, but everything turned out okay." She paused and took his hand, dragging him along the beach. Some thoughts demanded movement to be worked through. "We had a few weeks to pretend life was blissful, but we both know that danger is a constant part of our lives. Even here."

Q shook his head. "I feel so guilty for dragging you into this mess. We're supposed to be on our honeymoon–"

"Shush." She stopped. "*Liebling*, don't get so worked up. It wasn't your fault, and," she tilted her head to the side, "I love you, and I cannot imagine my life without you. I would rather die by your side than live without you."

Q turned her into his arms and kissed her with as much passion as desperation. They were both breathless when their lips parted and he said, "I want out."

"Out?" Her heart constricted, and a shiver ran down her spine as she leaned back in his arms to explore his blue eyes.

"The intelligence work. I want to stop."

Hilde breathed again.

After considering his words for a moment, she asked, "Would you be able to look me in the eyes every single day, or – more importantly – be able to look at yourself in the mirror, if you stopped?"

Q rubbed his chin, considering her question for a long moment. "Probably not." He looked out to sea and then asked quietly, "But what do I do about the Generalfeldmarschall? I sure don't want to work for the Ministry of War, but I don't see any way out."

Hilde nodded. "You probably don't have a choice. You'll have to go and at least talk to the man once we're back in Berlin."

"But I don't want to work for him," Q insisted.

"I know." She reached up and caressed his cheek. Q had a tendency to overthink things. "You'll go and meet with the man and then see how to continue from there."

"But–"

"No buts. In this case, it's best to take things day by day. We don't know what the future brings, and by the time we're back in Berlin, he may already have forgotten about the job offer." She didn't believe in her own words.

"You're right, my love. What would I do without you?"

She grinned. "Sit in some lab working on some important invention?"

"You know me too well."

***

The next morning, they woke up to a grey sky. Dark stormy clouds loomed on the horizon. It was their first day of bad weather since they'd left the Alps. But Q was determined to not let anything ruin their honeymoon – not the meeting with the Generalfeldmarschall and certainly not a thunderstorm.

He suggested spending the day at the most luxurious hot spa in town. While their hotel also offered a small pool, the town spa boasted several basins with different temperatures.

They entered the establishment through an ancient portal, and once inside, Hilde gasped at the sight. The original Roman architecture had been lovingly reconstructed. The main bath was surrounded by a walkabout covered in colorful tiles. While the pool was open-air, the walkabout featured a richly decorated roof, resting on sturdy columns with the heads of Roman Gods overlooking the area.

From the walkabout, several openings led to smaller private baths in different sizes and shapes, each one more elaborate than the next. The boiling hot thermal water bubbled through a set of open channels, flowing into the stone pools. The farther the water had to travel, the colder the receiving bath was.

Q and Hilde climbed into a heart-shaped pool. She reclined in the bath, tipped her head back, and waved a hand towards Q. "Where is the slave girl that is supposed to wash my hair?"

Q looked around the small area with a frown upon his face. "What are you talking about?"

Hilde giggled as she explained herself. "This looks so real, I was envisioning what life must have been like during the Roman and Greek empires. I'm a Roman lady with a multitude of servants at my beck and call."

Q laughed at these silly romantic and sentimental games. "You do have a vivid imagination."

"Right now I'm waiting for my servant to help me get ready to receive my lover because my husband is always traveling to countries far away."

"That I cannot accept," he said and tickled her in response.

Before Hilde could reply, Luise and Werner appeared in the entrance. Luise spotted them and came over, sliding into the hot water beside them. "Ahhh, aren't these Roman baths wonderful?"

Q and Hilde exchanged a look, and he said dryly, "Yes, they were." *Until you arrived.*

As Werner entered the pool, Q breathed against a constricting wall around his chest. Werner, though, grinned jovially at him. "The Roman Empire perished, but the Third Reich will prevail a thousand years. Our legacy will be even more glorious than those of the Greeks and the Romans."

Q nodded and added with a serious voice. "I believe generations to come will remember Hitler and his doings." He glanced over to Hilde, who'd been hogged by a chatty Luise. She rolled her eyes in his direction, and he raised his voice, "My love, your cheeks are reddening. We'll have to get you out of the hot water." With an apologetic glance to Werner and Luise, he added, "My wife is very susceptible to the heat."

As pleasantly as possible, they said their goodbyes, then hurried to the changing rooms and left the town spa. Back at the hotel, Hilde said, "We need to leave. Soon."

"Luise seems quite taken with you."

"And Werner likewise with you. If we stick around a few more days, we could all become best friends," Hilde said with a twist to her mouth.

Q chuckled. "I can see how eager you are for that to happen." He exhaled a long breath, going through all the possibilities before finally nodding. "We'll leave first thing in the morning."

While it was the wise thing to do, Q also wanted to stay until he was able to meet with the Russian contact. Unfortunately, he had no means to let him know where they were headed.

Chapter 9

Hilde and Q left the next morning, taking a bus inland to a small village located at the bottom of Mount Etna, a volcano on the east coast of Sicily. It was a tiny and peaceful place in the mountains and soon enough they returned to their blissful honeymoon state.

The Generalfeldmarschall was as quickly forgotten as the danger of Q's clandestine intelligence work. Some days later, they decided to walk up to the crater of the volcano. It was a very strenuous hike, and yet so beautiful.

After every turn, another beautiful view greeted them, each one more breathtaking than the one before. Below them lay green fields with blooming yellow bushes, and in the distance, the dark blue Mediterranean with a few white boats bobbing on the waves. The blue sky was a shade lighter than the ocean and cotton ball clouds flocked to the horizon.

As they neared the top of the volcano, a strong smell of sulfur greeted them and Hilde covered her mouth and nose with the thin scarf she'd tied over her hair before leaving that morning. "We must be almost to the top."

"I believe so," Q said.

Ten minutes later, they were gingerly peering over the edge of a cliff at the red, glowing lava several hundred feet below. The view from that height was amazing, and after glimpsing their fill of the bubbling guts of the mountain, they retreated a short distance away to enjoy the view of the valley below.

The mountain rumbled like a man with an empty stomach and Hilde jerked up. "Please, Q, let's hike down."

Q chuckled but obeyed when he saw the fear in her eyes. "Okay, let's go. I don't think it'll erupt anytime soon, though. The last big eruption occurred nine years ago and a smaller one in 1931. Geologists believe the volcano is in recess for at least another five years."

On their hike up, she'd only had eyes for the beautiful land and seascape, but on their way down, Hilde noticed the evidence of the big eruption in 1928. Lava had spilled from the mouth of the volcano and flowed down the mountainside on its way to the ocean – swallowing an entire village.

Hilde shuddered, and Q paused to wrap his arms around her. "There's no need to worry."

She wasn't so sure about that but tried a brave smile and pointed at the path of destruction the now cooled lava had left in its inky path. "I think everyone is wrong. The earth is rumbling like an angry bear, ready to spit out a load of death and destruction."

"You're exaggerating." Q tried to appease her.

"I'm not, and you know it," she insisted. "We're sitting on a barrel of explosives, just waiting for someone to ignite the fuse."

Q looked confused at her. "You're not talking about the volcano, are you?"

Tears wetted her eyes as she shook her head, trying to keep her voice steady. "War is coming. It's inevitable."

"Sadly, I believe you're right." He took her hand as they continued their hike down.

"Look at the desolate landscapes the lava left behind. Much like a moonscape." Not that any human had – or ever would – set foot on the moon.

Q helped her down a steep part of the mountain before he answered, "A war will be worse than this." She knew he was fifteen when the Great War ended.

After a pause, he continued, "While I've never been on the battlefield, I've heard enough stories from my older brothers to imagine the destruction. And with all the newly invented weapons, the coming war will be even more destructive."

Hilde shuddered at the thought that her entire country or maybe all of Europe might look like this stretch of devastated land on the slopes of Mount Etna. It was best not to go down that road, but to concentrate on the present.

Climbing up had been hard, but going down wasn't proving to be much easier. Two hours later, they reached the road again and stopped to rest their strained knees.

She took a big gulp from their water bottle, then leaned against Q. "I couldn't possibly have wished for a better life companion than you."

He kissed her nose. "I love you, Hildelein. I've loved you from the first moment I saw you in the movie theatre, and after three years, I'm still amazed that every day my love for you has grown even more."

She hugged him tight, lost in her thoughts. She didn't regret her decision to marry him, even if it meant exposing herself to danger. His intelligence work was honorable, and with every passing day, she was more convinced that the Nazis were out to destroy the entire world. Someone had to stop them. And if Q could be a small spoke in the wheel, she'd be proud and happy – with him.

Still, the thought of returning to Berlin terrified her. She sighed. "I wish we didn't have to go back."

Q was thoughtful for several minutes before suggesting, "We could stay in Italy."

Hilde stared at him, trying to process the implications of his words. "You would really consider such an idea?"

"Yes. The situation in Germany will only get worse. Right now, we're safer than we might ever be again."

They continued to discuss the possibility of never going back to Germany, but the idea was only that – an idea. Neither of them were truly serious about it.

When they'd almost reached the village, Q stopped when he spotted a lone man coming up the mountainside. "Stay here for a moment," he urged Hilde, putting a hand on her arm as he waited to get a better look at the man coming towards them.

Hilde squinted her eyes and then gasped. "Isn't that the Russian agent you were supposed to meet with?"

"It is. It would seem that Sicily is not so big after all."

***

An hour later, Q left his wife at the hotel room to get cleaned up and changed for dinner and promised to return soon. Just outside the village, Q met the agent, who introduced himself as – yet another -- Pavel, and they embarked on a walk through the fields.

"I still can't believe you found me."

"That's my job," the man said with a smirk. "Thanks again for warning me about von Blomberg. Now that your wife is safely back at the hotel, will you tell me what you discussed with him?"

Q couldn't be sure, but he believed he heard suspicion in the agent's voice. "He offered me a job."

"A job?" Pavel asked open-mouthed.

"Yes, he wants me to work for him at the Ministry of War. I declined."

"Are you crazy?"

Now it was Q's turn to drop his jaw. "Why? No! I can't possibly work for him, now can I?"

Pavel shook his head. "This is quite unusual, but it's a perfect opportunity. Think about all the intelligence you can gather from inside the Ministry of War!"

Q hadn't thought about that. What Pavel said made sense, but he didn't like the idea one bit. To work with the enemy – day in, day out. No. No. And no.

"I don't think I could do that. I'd be afraid I'd blow my cover at the first opportunity."

The agent scrutinized him. "Maybe you're right. But you should definitely think about it." He handed him a slip of paper with the name of Harro Schulze-Boysen and a telephone number.

"Who is this?"

"He's the leader of a communist resistance group."

"Military?" Q asked. He'd heard the name but couldn't immediately place his affiliation.

"Air Force. He's managed to maintain contact with the Soviet Union and the American authorities and has been warning both countries about the threats of war coming from within Germany."

Q took the paper and tucked it into his pocket. "I'll contact Schulze-Boysen, even though I believe working alone is safer."

"Not in this case. You must join with others who feel the same way you do and are working on orchestrating the demise of the Hitler regime. It will not be easy, but there is strength in numbers. Remember that."

"I will. Do you have any news from Germany?"

The agent shrugged. "Nothing special. On the surface, Germany and the Soviet Union appear to be on friendly terms. But the suspicion is high on both sides."

"This I know," Q said.

After discussing Stalin and how he was ruining the ideas of the November Revolution, Pavel gave him a last warning. "You need to be careful once you return to Germany. War is in the air, more so now than ever. It's no longer safe for you to visit the Soviet trade mission. We will contact you from now on."

"How will I know it's your people?" Q rubbed his chin.

The Russian narrowed his eyes, thinking, then broke into a broad smile. "Ask them if the hike up Mount Etna is strenuous. The answer will be, 'Not if you intend it at night.'"

Q almost choked on that hilarious sentence. "I will certainly remember that."

Chapter 10

Several weeks later, it was the end of summer, and Q and Hilde returned to Berlin. After spending four months in Italy and Switzerland, they felt like a distant relative who's the only one to notice how much a child has changed and how many new things it has learned while they were gone.

Much in contrast to the relaxed and peaceful atmosphere on their honeymoon, the atmosphere in the German capital was dire, to say the least. They felt the steady decline of everything "good and human" at every step. Swastika flags hung out of the windows, reminding the passers-by of who ruled the country. Open harassment on the streets by violent Brownshirts who didn't even attempt to hide their abuse.

Anyone and everyone could become the victim of scorn and maltreatment by SS or SA officers roaming the streets, but the Jews had to take the biggest share of vile persecution.

During the last few months, a strict racial segregation had been implemented throughout Germany. Jews were no longer allowed in the public parks, swimming pools, libraries, and basically any place people would spend their leisure time.

The Nazis had even gone so far as to segregate the compartments on the trains and buses, and during rush hour or in certain parts of the city, Jews weren't allowed the use of any public transportation at all. Q wondered how they were supposed to go to work.

He decided to check up on his friend Jakob Goldmann, from whom he hadn't heard since before they left on their honeymoon. But when Q paid a visit to Jakob's apartment in the center of Berlin, he didn't live there anymore. The landlady recognized Q from when he'd sublet a room from Jakob. She seemed to be uneasy as she explained that she'd had to terminate Mr. Goldmann's lease because she couldn't afford to do business with *those* persons.

Q thanked her and left, fuming inside about the injustice. The landlady had repeatedly praised Jakob for being such a good tenant. Quiet, clean, and always paying on time. And now he was considered undesirable because he belonged to *those* persons. He fisted his hand and punched the air, murmuring curse words under his breath.

I'm not going to give up. Ever.

The next day, he contacted Harro Schulze-Boysen and arranged to meet with him two weeks later. Schulze-Boysen picked him up with his Mercedes limousine at a busy intersection near the Reichstag. He'd been briefed by Pavel and knew Q's history. He explained the ways his own organization worked and then said, "Doctor Quedlin, I'd be more than happy to integrate you in our resistance network."

Q hesitated, because working alone definitely had its merits. "I already told Pavel that I'm not entirely convinced it's safe or prudent to liaise too closely."

Schulze-Boysen furrowed his brows. "We have an extensive network of resources at our disposal. And with your connections to the science world, we could distribute our leaflets much broader."

Leaflets? Q didn't believe distributing Anti-Nazi leaflets was a suitable way to end the terror regime. "I still believe it's safer for both of us not to work together, except in emergencies. But may I ask your advice in another affair?"

"Sure." Schulze-Boysen's mouth twitched, showing his bemusement.

"Generalfeldmarschall von Blomberg has extended a job offer to me, and I need to find a way out."

The bemused smile disappeared, and Schulze-Boysen's jaw dropped nearly to the floor. "What?"

Q explained the situation, and his counterpart seemed to grow more pleased by the minute.

"That is brilliant. Brilliant," Schulze-Boysen said, turning the steering wheel. "You absolutely have to take von Blomberg up on this offer. This is a golden opportunity. Think about all the intelligence you can gather working directly for the Ministry of War."

Q's stomach churned at the thought of inventing weapons for the *Wehrmacht*, the German army, "You don't understand what that would entail. I would have to betray everything I stand for. Day after day. Everyone around me – including myself – has to believe I'm a die-hard Nazi. I'm not sure I could hold up that façade for long." He paused and zoomed in on Schulze-Boysen. "I have no idea how you can stomach it."

The other man laughed. "You get used to it. It's like wearing a coat. One I take off as soon as I reach my home."

"I don't think I could." Q shook his head.

"Well, at least consider it. It would be of great service for our cause."

"Agreed."

Schulze-Boysen stopped the Mercedes to let Q exit the car, and in the blink of an eye, the limousine disappeared around the corner of the street. Q didn't attempt to follow the automobile's path with his eyes, he was too busy making sure that nobody followed him on his way home.

Since his return to Berlin, looking over his shoulder had become a constant habit. But for the first time in weeks, he loped, and a kernel of hope entered his heart. All was not lost. There were more people willing to stand up and fight for their freedoms – he and Hilde were not alone.

***

Another week went by, and Q had thought long and hard about Schulze-Boysen's advice to accept the job offered by von Blomberg, but he couldn't bring himself to act upon it. Instead, he hoped the Generalfeldmarschall would forget all about the job offer he'd extended.

But unfortunately, towards the end of October 1937, that hope was crushed as two uniformed SS officers arrived at his office, demanding to talk with Q.

The sight of the despised Nazi officers sent icy chills down his spine, and the sealed letter with an official looking seal in the hands of one of them didn't help either. Was this how they delivered arrests nowadays?

"Heil Hitler!" the officer saluted, clicking his heels.

Q let out a tiny breath and forced himself to return the salutation with the same enthusiasm. "Heil Hitler! What can I do for you officers?"

"We have an important message for you and have been asked to return your answer to the Minister of War."

Q's knees almost sagged in relief. They hadn't been sent for his head – but for his brains. He accepted the letter, and retreated to his desk, pulling out a letter opener from under a pile of paper.

With two pairs of perplexed eyes fixated on the sharp object in his hand, he carefully opened the envelope and retrieved a single sheet of paper with the official letterhead of the Ministry of War.

He leaned against his desk and began to read, the letters dancing in front of his eyes.

Wilhelm Quedlin,

I trust you and your wife returned from your journey to Italy and you are ready to serve Führer and Fatherland by offering up your intellect and knowledge for the furtherment of our cause. The job I mentioned to you is still available, and

I know you have most likely been waiting for confirmation that my offer was valid.

Consider this letter that confirmation. I will expect to see you in my office on Monday at 11 a.m. to discuss the details of your service for the greater good.

Please present this letter to your current employer, should you need to excuse yourself for work.

Welcome aboard.

Werner von Blomberg

Q swallowed hard and raised his head to look into the curious eyes of the SS officers staring at him. "Officers, please let the Generalfeldmarschall know that it is my greatest pleasure to accept his invitation. I'm looking forward to meeting him at his office this coming Monday, eleven o'clock sharp."

The SS men clicked heels again and left the office, leaving Q with a dizzy feeling. He popped onto the swivel chair and dropped his forehead to his desk. Whether he wanted to or not, he'd soon be working for the devil himself.

A million thoughts stormed his brain, but it was the image of devastation he'd seen on the slopes of Mount Etna that stayed with him and churned his gut. How could he live with the certainty that thousands would be killed in the future with weapons invented by him?

***

Q arrived in front of the Ministry of War with time to spare. The impressive grey stone building overlooked the Landwehr Kanal, an artificial canal branching off from the Spree river.

At this time of year, the trees lining the river bank were entirely bare, having shed their leaves weeks ago. They stood erect, raising their empty branches into the sky like pointed index fingers warning about coming doom.

He entered through the big wooden portal. The door creaked like a crow as it closed behind him and the blood congealed in his veins. The huge entry hall oozed terror, and it took all his strength not to turn on his heel and run.

Q announced himself at the reception, invitation letter in hand, and a uniformed officer ushered him into von Blomberg's office and announced, "Sir, Doctor Quedlin is here."

Von Blomberg greeted him with the obligatory "Heil Hitler" and then sat again behind an impressive dark wooden desk. *Probably oak.* Behind him on the wall, the ubiquitous picture of Hitler and a swastika flag. Two smaller swastika flags adorned his desk, along with a picture of Luise and another woman.

Q's eyes widened as he took in von Blomberg's appearance. Before him didn't sit the jovial, good-humored man he'd met back in Italy, but a man with an ashen grey face and bloodshot eyes that testified to a great deal of stress and little sleep.

With consideration to the uniformed officer standing next to him, Q opted for the formal salutation, "Herr Generalfeldmarschall, you requested to see me?"

"Yes. Please have a seat." Von Blomberg gestured towards one of the empty chairs.

Q did as he was bidden, unable to shake the feeling that something was very wrong.

"Doctor Quedlin, thank you for coming." A slight pause. "Unfortunately, things have changed in the last forty-eight hours, and I am not able to discuss your employment at this time."

"Sir?" Q wasn't sure whether to be elated – or terrified.

Von Blomberg sighed and then pushed himself out of his armchair to pace the length of his office. "You will understand that I cannot go into details, as these are matters of national security."

Q nodded. "I absolutely understand, sir."

Just as Q stood to bid his goodbyes, von Blomberg turned to him and said in a low voice, "I am getting married in January. Come back early February."

Relief washed over Q. "I will do that. Congratulations on your wedding."

The Generalfeldmarschall accepted the well wishes with a grimace. "If only it was all cause for happiness."

Q took his leave, not wanting to hear an explanation for the minister's strange comment. In public speeches or on the international stage, Hitler always mentioned that he was more than willing to accommodate for peace, but the meeting with von Blomberg had given a different impression.

The Wehrmacht knows there will soon be war, and the only question is where, not when.

Back home, he told Hilde about the peculiar meeting with von Blomberg, and she beamed at him. "See. No reason to worry. You've just gained three months."

"Yes. But what then?" He rubbed his chin.

"*Liebling*, don't worry so much. A lot of water will flow under the bridge until February, and many things can happen."

He kissed her on the mouth. "What would I do without you, Hildelein?"

She giggled. "Worry yourself sick?"

***

The holidays came and went, and they kept watching for news of von Blomberg's marriage to Luise. It finally came the second week of January. Hilde broke the news to Q as she brought home a newspaper showing the picture of the newly married couple standing next to their marriage witnesses – commander-in-chief of the air force, Herman Göring, and the Führer himself.

But just two weeks later, more alarming news emerged. Von Blomberg had drawn the eyes of everyone towards himself and his new bride, eyes that only looked for the bad things. And Luise turned out to be one of those bad things.

Hilde and Q sat on the couch together as the news of Luise's criminal history hit the radio. "Shush," Hilde said and turned the volume up.

"...the 25-year old former typist and secretary has a long criminal record ranging from theft to impersonation to moral indecency, which apparently has been excused by our Führer because she promised betterment.

But the police came up with another, even graver offense. The entire nation is shocked to the bones by the horrific crimes she committed against decency and racial purity by posing for pornographic photos a few years back. Those unspeakable actions were further aggravated by the fact that those photos had been taken by a Jewish photographer this woman had been living together with..."

Hilde switched off the radio, because what followed was the usual bashing of Jews and the unspeakable "crime" of an Aryan woman mingling with a sub-human and thus impurifying the master race.

The scandal was fierce, and a few days later, Werner von Blomberg abdicated from all of his official functions, supposedly for health reasons.

"Can you believe an intelligent man in such a high-level position could trip over a woman?" Hilde asked.

"No. I thought he would have checked her background before marrying her."

Hilde grinned. "Well, on the bright side, you won't be keeping that second meeting with him, will you?"

Q nodded. "Definitely not. How was work for you today?"

Hilde shrugged. "It was fine."

She'd taken such a long leave of absence that she'd been afraid her position would no longer be available upon her return to the insurance company. But the opposite turned out to be true. "We have so many claims to process, the company is desperately seeking additional skilled staff."

"Same at the Biological Institute. We're swamped with research orders, but not enough men to do the work."

"Or women." Hilde pouted, and Q took her hand in his. "You know what I mean. It's actually ironic. A few years back, the Nazis coerced women to stay home and raise children, and now that they need the men for their war efforts, they change course and encourage the same women to come back to the factories."

Hilde leaned against Q's shoulder. "Erika has been promoted again. They've given her twice as many people to oversee, including the new accounting department staff."

"Congratulations. She must be doing good work."

Hilde rolled her eyes. "I believe it has more to do with her Party book than with the quality of her work."

"Oh, when did she join the Party?"

"About a month ago." Hilde sighed and turned to look into Q's eyes. "Erika is one of my best friends, but we have to be careful. Since she became enamored with that SS officer, she's changed."

"We will. Let's go to bed." Q stood and pulled Hilde from the couch. While doing her evening ablutions, she thought about her company. On the surface, nothing had changed. The economy was picking up, and everyone seemed to look forward to better times. But there was an ever-present underlying tension. People watched their words, careful not to accidentally make anti-Nazi or pro-Jewish comments.

It was too dangerous.

Chapter 11

Things in Europe were starting to unravel at an alarming rate. The Gestapo was quickly becoming one of the most feared groups in Berlin and across Germany. Luckily, Q hadn't been the focus of any of their investigations, but he couldn't say the same for some of his colleagues.

On March 12, 1938, completely different news surprised the German population. The long awaited war was over before it began.

Hitler had marched with his troops into Austria and declared his home country a federal state of Germany, which he now called *Großdeutsches Reich*, Great German Empire. And what happened? Nothing.

The cabinet of Nazi supporters in the Austrian government willingly agreed to the annexation, and all over Austria and Germany, spontaneous celebrations took place with people dancing in the streets.

Q couldn't help but wonder throughout the next days. Hitler's triumphal march to Vienna was accompanied by cheering and flower-throwing crowds. Did those people not know what awaited them?

It was a surreal occurrence and culminated in Hitler's enthusiastic speech in front of thousands of Austrians announcing the entrance of his native country into the German Empire.

Q wanted to puke. But apparently, he was the only one to think that way. As spring passed, Q found himself in a constant state of worry. Even his work at the Biological Reich Institute proved increasingly challenging. His area of expertise – plant protection – wasn't deemed *war important*. Q had thought this to be an advantage because the authorities wouldn't interfere with his research, but he soon found that was wishful thinking and the opposite was true.

He constantly had to justify his plant protection research, and more than once had been forced to stop the work, whether by lack of materials and funds or because he didn't get access to a vital piece of information that had been deemed a military secret.

More and more of his colleagues were forced to change the focus of their experimentation to fit the needs of the Third Reich and the war effort. It was only a matter of time until Q would have to oblige as well.

Biological warfare.

That was what the government wanted. New biological weapons to use against Germany's enemies.

The Nazis considered this research pertinent to winning an upcoming war and began to scrutinize the scientists more closely than in the past. Everyone had to produce a greater Aryan certificate, proof that parents and all four grandparents were Aryan. Q groaned as he remembered the months and months of struggle to get the required Catholic baptism certificate of his Hungarian grandmother when he needed the *Ariernachweis* to receive his marriage license one and a half years ago.

The scientists had been given four weeks to produce their respective Aryan certificates, and at the end of the month, all but one colleague had handed it in. Very few Jews were still allowed to work in critical industries, and that colleague was one of those unfortunate ones. The next day, the Gestapo stormed the building and dragged him from the facility.

According to the rumors, the poor fellow was half Jewish, enough for the Gestapo to consider him a threat to national security and treat him accordingly. Q and his colleagues pretended not to see or hear anything, going about their daily work, hoping they'd be left in peace.

But the nightmare wasn't over yet. More Gestapo officers arrived to thoroughly question all colleagues before anyone was allowed to leave for the day. Lined up in the large courtyard, they were led one by one to a small room for interrogation.

Q could barely breathe when his name was called out, and he followed the Gestapo officer with a wildly beating heart. It took his eyes a few moments to adjust from the bright sunlight in the courtyard to the dimly lit room. The office of one of the accountants. Now an important looking Gestapo man with soulless grey eyes and all the insignia of importance on his uniform resided behind the desk. Lower ranking officers flanked him on either side.

"Name and profession."

"Doctor Wilhelm Quedlin. Chemical engineer."

"Party book."

Q clenched his jaw to disguise a shiver. "I'm not a member of the Party."

The Gestapo man looked up, his stare boring into Q's skin like a red-hot iron rod. "Why not?"

Because I hate everything the Nazis stand for. Q raised his chin and returned the stare as steadfast as he was capable of. "Sir, I don't understand much of politics. My science is my life."

Apparently, this answer didn't satisfy the interrogator because it prompted a whole new set of questions about Q's loyalties, his activities, and his general opinion about the Führer and Fatherland.

Q answered all the questions as inauspiciously as he could, but at the umpteenth repetition, his temper broke through. "You are hindering my work. I need to return to my experiments."

No sooner had the words left his mouth than Q realized the foolish mistake he'd committed. He only had a very short amount of time – if any – to correct his error, and quickly apologized. "Gentlemen, I apologize for my outburst. I was in the middle of a time-critical experiment that is of the utmost importance to Germany and her people."

The Gestapo officer looked at his notes and then scoffed. "You work with plants. How can that be of vital importance to the Party?"

Q swallowed back his first response and calmly explained, "I'm working on orders from the highest authority on methods to increase agricultural production. Our Führer wants to assure that German people won't have to suffer through years of famine as we did during the Great War."

Judging by the pained expression on his face, the well-fed man behind the desk remembered all too well the terrible hunger he experienced two decades ago.

The palpable tension in the room eased up and Q lowered his head and waited.

"Well, then you better get back to work. We wouldn't want to interfere with the intention of our Führer."

"Thank you, sir," Q answered and turned to leave but was called back. "Doctor Quedlin, consider joining the Party. Questioning would have been unnecessary if you'd had the proper paperwork."

Q thanked him for the suggestion and tamped down on the hatred he carried for everything Nazi. He went back to his laboratory, hiding his fear as best as he could. He knew it had been a very thin line that had kept him from being arrested today, and he vowed to do nothing that might draw more scrutiny from the Gestapo.

He feared for his life. Like everyone these days.

Once he was sure the Gestapo had taken their leave, he packed up his briefcase and headed home. At the sound of the slamming door, Hilde came from the small kitchen with a towel in her hands and asked, "What's wrong, my love?"

"I can't take it anymore," he burst out, tossing his briefcase to the floor and sinking down into the couch.

"Can't take what?" Hilde queried, coming to sit beside him.

"The Nazis. The war preparations. Germany! We have to leave the country if we are to ever be happy again."

"Leave? But where would we go?" Alarm was written on her face.

"America. They appreciate scientists there. I have a future there. We do. What do we have here? Nothing but more fear and censorship."

"But America is so far away." Hilde seemed so small as she sank deeper into the couch beside him, and he wanted to console her.

Q put an arm around her shoulders. "I know. And this is very sudden. But we wouldn't be alone. My cousin Fanny married an American dentist a few years back and went to live with him in Forest Hills, New York. I'm sure she would be willing to help us."

Hilde said nothing, and after a day or two, the discussion naturally slipped to the sidelines as more pressing matters came forward.

Chapter 12

Hilde stepped out of the bathroom. She should be excited about this evening's event, but she was having trouble mustering up any enthusiasm. Her company had made it possible for all of their employees, and a guest, to watch the movie *Olympia – Fest der Schönheit/Fest der Völker* by Leni Riefenstahl in the Ufa-Palast.

The movie was all the rage in Berlin – a beautiful homage to the Olympic Games – Games of Beauty and Games of Nations, held in Berlin two years earlier. Normally, Hilde would be excited about such an outing as Leni Riefenstahl made excellent and captivating movies. But Leni was also a very good friend with Hitler and lately all of her movies had been nothing more than blatant propaganda for the regime.

"You look lovely, Hilde," Q complimented her, folding up the newspaper he'd been reading and getting to his feet as she stepped into the room.

She gave him a smile and then smoothed a hand down the skirt of her dress. It was a very smart outfit, navy blue with large white polka dots scattered all over it. A small ruffled collar with a tie combined with the pencil skirt design and white jacket completed the outfit. She pulled on her gloves after pinning the navy blue hat to her hair and then turned to look at Q. "Are you sure we need to go?"

"If you don't go, it will certainly be noticed, and the idea is to keep a low profile. It's better to show up and make sure the right people notice you and then leave as soon as it is practical, rather than stirring up questions as to why you were absent."

"I know all of that," she sighed, "I'm just tired of being bombarded by Nazi propaganda at every turn."

Q put his hand on the small of her back. "I understand that, but this is what we need to do now. We'll watch the movie, attend the reception for a short time and then leave."

Hilde nodded and stepped out of the apartment while he held the door for her. They took his automobile to the Ufa-Palast, and Hilde made an effort to smile and act like she was enjoying herself as colleagues greeted her and Q.

During the break, Q and Hilde left the building through a side entrance to fill their lungs with fresh air. Some of her colleagues followed suit. When Q stopped and stared off into the distance, a peculiar stiffness filled his body. Hilde whispered, "What's wrong?"

"Come with me and pretend nothing's out of the ordinary," Q breathed into her ear and led her around a corner while kissing her neck. Hilde giggled. After being married almost two years, he sure didn't need to take her into a dark alley to kiss her.

But as soon as they were out of sight of her colleagues, a man stepped from the shadows and Q released her to greet him. "Jakob Goldmann. I was worried sick about you. Your landlady–"

Jakob pulled him in for a friendly hug. "Q, it is so good to see you. I didn't want to get you into trouble, but when I heard that Hilde's company rented the Ufa-Palast tonight, I hoped to see you," Jakob said, stepping back and giving Hilde a smile.

"You look awful!" Hilde said, and it was true. Since she'd last seen him a year ago, he'd aged at least twenty years. His shoulders slumped forward and at twenty-eight, he already sported salt-and-pepper hair. Lines sharp enough to be seen in the dimly lit alley had furrowed his face and given him the look of a broken man.

"What have you been up to?" Q wanted to know.

Jakob shook his head. "Things are not good. Each day life for us Jews gets a little harder. After my landlady terminated my lease contract, I had to move in with my parents."

Hilde felt awful for him. He'd been one of Q's best friends, and she knew that Q felt guilty for not having kept contact with him after they returned from Italy. She put a hand on Jakob's arm and asked. "How are your parents?"

His eyes glistened. "Dead. Both of them."

She gasped, covering her mouth with her hand as tears sprang to her eyes. Jakob looked at her and tried a small smile. "Don't cry for me."

She nodded, swallowing back her tears because she could tell that he was barely keeping his own emotions together.

"My mother was forced to return from retirement. The Nazis said she was a work-shy parasite, and sent her to work in a factory producing military goods."

"That's horrible!" Hilde shouted, righteous anger building in her breast. Jakob's mother was a fragile person and anyone who'd met her knew she wasn't fit to work.

Q took her arm and said, "Shush. We don't want your colleagues to hear us."

Jakob cleared his throat. "Mom died one week later from a heart attack. With her fragile condition, the hard work and long hours were too much for her."

"Oh, Jakob! I'm so sorry," Hilde said, losing the battle to keep her tears hidden. She ducked her head and surreptitiously wiped them away.

"And your father?" Q wanted to know, placing a comforting arm around Hilde's shoulders.

"My father stopped talking the day my mother died. Not one word. When the Nazis found out, they took him away, supposedly to a mental home. I wasn't allowed to visit, and they wouldn't even tell me where he was. A few days later, a letter arrived to inform me my father was dead."

Hilde was openly crying now, and Q clasped his friend's shoulder. "I'm so sorry, my friend. You need to leave Germany before it's too late."

"But–"

"No buts. Now that your parents are both gone, there's nothing left to keep you here. You must go if you want to survive."

"Where should I go? All of the European countries have imposed quotas to receive Jewish immigrants from Germany."

Q tilted his head, thinking. "The farther away, the better. Go to America. They are in need of young and brilliant scientists like you."

"Do you really think they'll give me a visa?"

"You'll never know if you don't try," Q urged his friend. "Do it for me. So I'll know you're safe."

Hilde wiped her cheeks and added, "And if you're successful, we might come and visit you."

Jakob chuckled. "You two are good friends. I'll think about it."

Too soon, it was time for Q and Hilde to slip back inside the cinema before anyone was the wiser. Jakob hugged them both once more and promised to find a way to let them know what was happening with him. Before entering the cinema, Q waited while Hilde visited the bathroom and splashed some cool water on her face.

When she returned, she felt only slightly better, and even more anxious for the evening to come to an end.

Chapter 13

Three months later, Hilde and Q came home to find a letter from Q's cousin Fanny in America. She told them about her life in Forest Hills, New York and asked about the well-being of the other family members. The letter ended with an invitation to visit her and her husband for a few weeks.

"What do you think, Hilde?" Q asked. "Should we try to get travel visas for America?"

"That sounds exciting," Hilde answered. "I'll get three weeks of leave next summer."

Over dinner, they made plans for their upcoming vacation across the ocean and Q teased Hilde about her excitement.

Just as they finished eating dinner and Hilde was washing the dishes in the kitchen, the telephone rang. Q answered it. "Wilhelm Quedlin."

"It's Jakob."

"Jakob, it's good to hear from you." Q gripped the telephone receiver tighter. Since he'd last seen his friend at the Ufa-Palast, he'd only heard bad news. Jakob had been disposed from his job, repeatedly harassed by Brownshirts when running errands, and he'd been denied visas by several European countries.

"I have good news," Jakob said, and Q released his breath. "I received my visa to emigrate to America. The final paperwork arrived this afternoon, and I'm already booked on a ship out of Hamburg three days from now, on November tenth, to travel to New York."

"That's great news! Congratulations!"

"Thanks. I'm so relieved. This ship will take me to safety. Finally." Jakob hesitated. "Q?"

"What, my friend?"

"I hate to ask...but the situation with the trains...do you think there's any way you could drive me to Hamburg?"

"Of course I'll drive you down. It's the least I can do."

"Thank you. It means a lot. I need to take care of a few more things, given that I most likely won't come back..." Jakob's voice broke.

Q could feel the pain in his friend's heart. It wasn't easy to leave everything behind and embark on an uncertain adventure. "Don't worry. You'll do just fine. And you'll find yourself a nice young woman soon enough over there."

Jakob tried a chuckle. "I'm sure I will. It's not safe for you to come to my place. Can you meet me by the train station? Seven o'clock Thursday morning."

"Sure. See you then and take care." Q hung up the phone just as Hilde exited the kitchen, drying her hands with a towel.

"Who were you talking to?" she asked.

"Jakob. He's got a visa for America." Q took Hilde in his arms and whirled her around, then set her back on her feet. "He asked me to drive him to the harbor in Hamburg on Thursday."

"Oh. That's wonderful. We might even be able to visit him there next summer." Q loved to see the genuine smile on her face. Maybe the first in many weeks. But then, she wrinkled her nose.

"What's wrong, *Liebling*?" Q asked.

"Nothing. I just thought…if I ask for two days' leave, I could come with you. We could visit my family for the weekend."

"That's a terrific idea. We'll do that." Q agreed.

***

Thursday morning arrived, and Q and Hilde arrived at the allotted place in time, but Jakob never showed up.

"Where is he?" Hilde asked, worry in her voice.

"I don't know. This is unlike him. He's usually overly punctual."

They waited in the automobile and Q turned the radio on, searching for a musical program to help release some of the tension that was quickly building. Instead of a musical program, he could only find news report after news report. Giving up, he let the radio play and horror seeped deep into his body at what he heard.

Last night, November 9, 1938, the Nazi regime had launched a terror campaign against the Jewish people in both Germany and Austria. *Reichskristallnacht*, the Night of Broken Glass, as the radio speaker called it.

Q's stomach churned at the vivid detail of the violence that had occurred throughout the night. The radio speaker didn't even try to hide his enthusiasm as he recounted all the atrocities committed against the Jewish citizens. Ransacked homes. Sledgehammered businesses. Demolished schools. Burnt synagogues. Profaned graveyards. Hundreds of Jews murdered. Thousands arrested and sent to concentration camps.

"How did we not know this was happening?" Hilde asked, tears in her eyes.

"We don't live in an area where there are any Jews." Q's voice was barely audible.

"You don't think that something happened to Jakob? Did he live in a Jewish part of the city?"

Q nodded and immediately started the automobile. "Jakob was living in his parents' house. So yes, he lived in a Jewish quarter." He drove towards that part of the city, and as they passed by Jewish businesses and homes, the devastation was harrowing.

Deserted streets with bodies lying where they'd fallen. Smoldering fires. Q swallowed hard. "Hilde, this is probably not a good idea."

Hilde wiped her tears. "Don't you want to know?"

Q nodded, tears clogging his throat at the senseless acts of violence in plain view. "Maybe he needs our help. We have to get to his place."

They drove the rest of the way in silence. When the debris in the street made it impossible to drive any farther, he parked and opened the door for Hilde, and they picked their way towards the small house where Jakob's parents had lived.

Q took a deep breath before he pushed the door open and entered the hallway. Then he froze. Jakob lay at the bottom of the stairs, his lifeless eyes staring up at the ceiling, his skin swollen and battered, a pool of dried blood beneath his head.

He swallowed back the bile that rose in his throat and turned, intending to keep Hilde from seeing this, but he was too late. She took one look at Jakob's body and screamed. The windows in the staircase resonated with her voice and Q was afraid they'd burst.

He grabbed her by the waist and pulled her out of the building, burying her head against his chest in an effort to calm her down. "Shush!"

Hilde's muffled screams filled the air, and Q looked up and down the street, fearing upset neighbors – or worse – to bombard them. But no one came running. Q noticed a curtain moving in one of the buildings, but the street remained abandoned.

Soon, Hilde's screams eased into sobbing, and he wished he could release his emotions in the same way. Despite the grief, his eyes stayed dry. The weight of guilt for his friend's death pressed on his shoulders, making it difficult to breathe. *I wasn't there to help him. If I only had urged Jakob to leave the country earlier, he'd be safe on the ship by now. I should have made more of an effort to keep in touch with him, to protect him. He was my best friend...*

"Don't do this." Hilde looked up at him with puffy tear-stained eyes, clasping his cheeks in her hands.

"Do what?" Q asked, his voice husky.

"I know you. You're feeling guilty for what happened. But there was nothing you could have done to prevent it."

"I could have tried–"

"Tried what? To stop the Nazis from looting?"

Q nodded. She was right, but it didn't make things any easier. He looked back towards the building. The windows were broken, furniture was smashed, belongings were strewn about...it looked like a war zone.

"I want to say a prayer for him. You don't have to join me."

"Of course I will, he was my friend, too," Hilde answered, straightening her spine and her resolve.

He stepped back inside the building, keeping Hilde close to his side and said a quick prayer for Jakob's soul. It was the only thing they could do. He wished there was some way to organize a proper burial, but under the circumstances, it was impossible. As cruel as it was, he and Hilde had to return to their automobile, leaving Jakob lying there at the bottom of the stairs.

Q drove them back to their place, glancing at Hilde frequently. Her face had turned ghostly white, and she was awfully quiet, sitting perfectly still, except for her hands. She was worrying her fingers to the point where he finally reached over and covered them, knowing she was going to injure herself if she continued.

"Hilde?"

"I want out. I just want away from all of this."

Q squeezed her hands. "We should drive to Hamburg as planned. It will get us away from Berlin for a few days, and your sisters will distract us."

"Without Jakob? Who should have embarked on the ship to start a new life..."

"We have to move on, Hilde. As hard as it is, there is nothing we can do for Jakob. But we can help ourselves by giving our minds a small reprieve from the grief."

Hilde nodded, settled into the seat and closed her eyes.

"Sleep, *mein Liebling*, and dream about your sisters," he said.

The trip to Hamburg wasn't the joyous event they had originally planned, but one of sorrow and worry. Hilde's family was equally agitated upon their arrival. Hamburg had experienced the same outbursts of violence as Berlin, and while the quarter of the Dremmer family had been spared, they'd heard the radio reports and worried.

But Carl and Emma had made it a rule not to make any negative comments in front of their teenage daughters because they were afraid Julia or Sophie might blurt out something inappropriate at school.

Nobody wanted to get caught criticizing the Nazi regime as that was a sure way to become the next victim. Thus it was only in the evenings after the girls had gone to bed that Q and Hilde felt comfortable voicing their concerns to her parents.

"I just don't see how these atrocities can continue," Q stated.

Carl nodded. "I agree with you, but what are the options? The Jews are powerless to fight back, and anyone even suspected of showing them sympathy is likely to be treated as a traitor."

"But where will our nation end up if everyone just stands by and turns a blind eye?"

Carl stared for long moments at Q and Hilde before he said, "You two are young and without responsibilities. But I just turned fifty-three and have a wife and two teenagers depending on me. I may not agree with what the Nazis are doing, but I can't afford to battle them."

Q didn't want to go down that route and changed the topic of the discussion. "A few days ago, we received a letter from my cousin Fanny in America. She invited us over to visit."

Emma joined the discussion. "You should definitely go while you still can. Once you have children, travelling that far won't be so easy."

Hilde giggled. "Q's mother gave us the same advice before we embarked on our honeymoon." Then she kissed Q lightly on the cheek and whispered in his ear, "It sounds like everyone is waiting for grandchildren."

Q smiled. He was getting the same impression. "We were planning to visit Fanny next summer."

"You shouldn't wait too long," Carl said and lit a cigarette, offering one to Q. "Who knows how long it will be before we are at war, and you won't be able to leave the country for leisure trips."

Q nodded. It had been time-consuming to secure the visa and papers for their honeymoon in Europe, how much more challenging would it be two years later to travel to America? "We'll send a letter to Fanny right away."

Chapter 14

The *Kristallnacht* was only the first of many terror campaigns against the Jewish people in both Germany and annexed Austria. Q was in a constant state of alert, a premonition of worse things to come looming in his subconscious.

His faith in the good of humanity had been severely shattered as he witnessed time after time what people could do with their hatred. Nothing was the way it was before, and Q was appalled by the actions of his compatriots.

As New Year arrived, he was still dealing with guilt over Jakob's death, moping around without finding joy in even the things he liked most.

"Q, you have to stop this. You are not responsible for Jakob's death," Hilde said once and again, but Q refused to listen. His mood had been steadily declining, and he was slipping into a deep depression. The only thing to lighten his mood was planning their upcoming visit to his cousin Fanny in America.

"What is the weather like in Forest Hills?" Hilde asked as they sat over dinner.

"June through August are the hottest months of the year. Fanny wrote the temperatures can be well above 80° Fahrenheit, which is close to 30° Celsius."

Hilde smiled. "I'll need summer dresses. Maybe I should start to do some shopping?"

Against his will, Q had to chuckle. If life was only that easy. He doubted Hilde could buy summer dresses right then. Not in January and not in a Germany singularly focused on war.

Without warning, his good humor turned into anger, and his frustration burst out. "The whole damn nation is focused on war. Every industry has been re-purposed to keep the war machine running smoothly. There's no liberty to develop me scientifically. All my work is redirected to research war-relevant things they want to use as weapons."

Q pushed over an empty glass as he talked himself into a rage.

He went on, "Can you believe those narrow-minded officials in charge laughed at the inventions Otto and I presented them several years ago. And now they are feverishly trying to produce something similar, and yet inferior."

Hilde moved the glass out of his reach before she filled it with water. "I thought you were relieved that the government didn't buy your inventions?"

"I was. I am." Q sighed. "I couldn't have lived with the knowledge that my inventions are used to kill innocent people simply because of their heritage. But it still hurts that those arrogant men refused my work and think they can do better on their own." He paused and ran a hand through his hair. "And you know what is the worst?"

Hilde looked reluctant to ask. "No. What?"

"I used to think a weapon as being neither good nor bad, it just is. But humans will always abuse them. Allow any of those testosterone-driven lads free use of a weapon and he will use it against his fellow human. Hatred, fear, and the sense of power will do that to him."

Hilde put a hand on his arm. "You're exaggerating, my love. Mankind is not that bad, and things surely will get better."

"No, they won't." Q buried his head in his hands, the evil of the entire world weighing him down.

"Maybe we should look at extending our trip to America to several months, rather than just visiting for a few weeks?" Hilde suggested.

He looked up. Surprised. A zing of euphoria rushed through his veins. "You would? I mean... our trip to America is the one thing to make me happy, but whenever I think about having to leave and come back here, I fall back into my depressive state of mind."

"Then we should apply for green cards in America," Hilde said.

Q looked at her with wide eyes. She was the one to resist that idea when he first mentioned it. But so many things had changed during the last year. The situation in Germany was hopeless. Hitler would never back down until he got everything he wanted. Austria. Sudeten territories. What would be next on his list?

"Isn't that being cowardly to use the easy way out and run?" he whispered.

"No. You've done so much already." Hilde put a hand on his arm." Maybe you'll be of better use against the Nazi regime from outside, where you can concentrate on your research work. Like this echo-sound system to locate ships and airplanes you told me about."

He'd almost forgotten about his echo-sound theories. The Royal Air Force had shown interest but had asked him to deliver a working prototype, not just theories on paper.

"Maybe you're right, and it's not cowardly to emigrate. I guess, I'm not cut out to be a hero."

"You are my hero," Hilde said and circled the table to sit on his lap. For the first time since finding Jakob's body, Q was filled with hope and excitement at the possibilities that lay before them.

He held her close and said, "Let's go to the embassy first thing in the morning and turn in our applications for a green card."

Chapter 15

Several weeks later, they received a letter with the denial of their requested travel visa. The reason stated was that green card applicants couldn't also hold a travel visa. Probably out of fear that those persons would simply not return when their allowed time was up.

Q and Hilde were suitably disappointed, but still hopeful. The drawing for the green card lottery would take place later in the year, and they decided to travel then. Meanwhile, they tried to live as normal a life as possible.

When *Gone with the Wind* came to the movie theater, Hilde convinced Q to take her to the premiere. It had occupied the headlines for weeks, and all her friends wanted to see Scarlet O'Hara and Rhett Butler. It was a welcome distraction from dull reality.

Hilde was wearing a new two-piece dress with a fitted, pencil skirt, and a fitted jacket that fanned out below her waist like a short skirt. The long sleeves and deep burgundy color gave her skin a healthy glow. The matching three-inch heels made her feel like Scarlett herself.

She giggled and daydreamed about a dashing Rhett Butler carrying her away on his horse. She couldn't understand why Q thought the movie was cheesy.

"You truly didn't like it?" Hilde asked as they walked home.

"No. Scarlett was a selfish brat."

"Yes, but she endured so much, didn't you feel even a modicum of sympathy for her?" Hilde pouted.

"Not really. I agree that war is awful and she lost so much, but that doesn't excuse her behavior. Not in my book."

Hilde sighed and shook her head. "We'll just have to agree to disagree."

"Very well." Q paused and looked at her shoes. "Are you sure you want to walk home in those? We can always take a tram."

"No. It's such a lovely evening, and I need some fresh air."

"You look beautiful," he said, pulling her close to his side.

"Thank you." She tucked her handbag beneath her elbow and slipped her gloved hand in the crook of her husband's arm. The small hat she wore had a piece of netting that fell over the top to just below her eyes. This kind of netting was the current fashion and seemed to be showing up on most of the new hats this year.

She looked up at her husband and grinned. "You're looking rather dashing yourself this evening."

Q grinned back at her. "I can't let you receive all of the admiring looks, now can I?"

Hilde fingered the fabric of his new linen suit in a light heather grey. The pants were cuffed at the bottoms, and a large lapel adorned the jacket that Q had buttoned only once, in the middle.

He'd paired the suit with a crisp white shirt and a white cravat tied around his neck, tucked into the neckline of the shirt. As they readied themselves for bed, she said, "You definitely could give Rhett Butler a run for his money in the looks department. Thanks for taking me to see the movie."

"Hmm. I might ask some favors in return." He pulled her into the bed beside him.

***

Hilde was still smiling the next day as she arrived at her office. She looked at her schedule to see she had a meeting with one of her biggest clients that morning. His industrial company produced lubricants and filters for machinery.

Herr Becker arrived, worrying his fingers and fidgeting on the seat she offered him. This was not his usual behavior.

"Herr Becker, thanks for coming. It's been a long time, and I wanted to go over those statistics with you. The number of occupational accidents in your Berlin factory has soared recently."

"Frau Quedlin." The sturdy man in his fifties looked at her like a schoolboy caught in mischief and folded his hands. "We have already implemented measures to decrease the number, if this is what worries you."

Hilde looked straight into his brown eyes, and Herr Becker evaded her glance. "I'm sure you did. But what strikes me as unusual is that our insurance company settles only a fraction of those accidents. Are you not satisfied with us anymore?"

Herr Becker lowered his head. "No, it's not that." His voice fell to a whisper. "The Berlin factory has been assigned one thousand new workers."

Hilde smiled, pleased for his growing success. "Congratulations. That's excellent news." When the man's face fell, and his eyes took on a pained expression, she lowered her voice and leaned closer. "It isn't good news?"

"Not really." He leaned over the desk and whispered, "They're Czech workers."

She still didn't understand. "And…?"

Herr Becker sighed. "Workers displaced from the occupied territories forced to work for the *Reich*."

Hilde gasped. "You don't mean…?"

He sighed again, misery flashing across his face. "No. Look. I'd rather employ people working out of free will, but I don't have much choice. The authorities have raised my production quota, and without those Czech workers, I cannot reach it. There's just no way to find one thousand workers on the market." The man leaned back, intently studying the tip of his shoes.

Hilde took a few moments to process his words. It didn't make sense. "I understand why your occupational accidents have gone up, but why did the claims go down at the same time?"

Herr Becker coughed. "Because we don't insure them. They're considered second class workers and get none of the benefits our own employees do." He was talking himself into a rage, and Hilde was glad that the colleague she shared the office with had called in sick for the day.

"Their working conditions are horrible. They get less payment and have to work longer hours. They have to do all the dangerous and dirty work, sometimes without the necessary instructions or protective gear. They live in camps. And the *Reichsarbeitsamt* requires me to give a weekly report on their performance and behavior. Anyone found lacking faces severe sanctions."

The blood left Hilde's face, and she felt a slight dizziness. "Sanctions?"

"Yes. The work office even provided me with special supervisors for them, and more than once, I saw one of the supervisors mistreating the workers. But my hands are bound. The only thing I can do is forbid punishment at the factory because of the implications for the general work safety. But what happens at the camp, I don't know. Some don't come back the next day."

Hilde stopped breathing altogether.

"If I don't reach the production quota, someone else will," Herr Becker added in a defeated voice.

Just then, her boss entered the room. Herr Becker jumped up and greeted the newcomer, "Heil Hitler."

"Herr Becker, I was told you were coming in today. How are those new workers doing?"

The despondency and complaints of a few moments ago changed before her eyes and Herr Becker answered with a loud and cheerful voice. "Having those workers has been a great addition to the cause. I can't thank the government enough for seeing the need and taking such prudent actions to help my company perform the best it can for the Reich."

"That is good to hear." Her boss glanced over at Hilde, and she quickly ducked her head. "Is Frau Quedlin taking care of your needs?"

Herr Becker readily came to her aide. "Yes, sir, she is an excellent representative of the company. Unfortunately, for your company, we aren't required to insure the new workers."

"I know. Don't worry about that. If you need anything else from us, don't be afraid to let Frau Quedlin know. We all need to do our best for the Reich. Have a good day." Hilde watched her boss leave the office and then bid her goodbyes to Herr Becker.

She probably should have been shocked, but everyone kowtowed to the Nazi ideals when pressed. *Including myself.* While she never openly praised the government, she had long ago stopped saying anything negative in regards to the Nazis, Third Reich, and Hitler. Like everyone here, she just wanted to survive.

Chapter 16

Denied.

Q stared down at the paper in his hands…his hopes and dreams burning to ashes. A letter from the United States Embassy with the lapidary message that his and Hilde's number hadn't been drawn in the green card lottery. But they were encouraged to apply again next year.

One year?

That seemed like an eternity given the current conditions. Hilde was staring at him, and he cleared his throat before re-reading the letter to her. He wasn't fooled by her attempt to put on a brave face. The disappointment was too obvious.

"Well, it looks like we won't be travelling to America this summer. Nor will we make a permanent move anytime soon."

Hilde's eyes welled with tears as she nodded and he took her hand in his. "Maybe we should take another trip to Italy?"

"Yes, that would be something. See the places we didn't on our honeymoon." Hilde leaned against his back, looping her arms around him, and he knew she longed for the blissful time they'd spent away from Germany.

"I'll request the travel visa tomorrow. I guess I need to write Fanny and let her know we won't be visiting this year after all." Then he stood and headed for his office to grab pen and paper.

It took him a few minutes to tamp down his disappointment before he sat down to write his cousin a letter.

Dearest Fanny,

I hope this letter finds you and your family in good health and spirits. I'm writing to bring you the unpleasant news that Hilde and I won't be visiting you this summer after all.

Fate has prevented us from taking the easy way out, as we did not get chosen in the lottery to receive green cards. I have to confess that Hilde and I were looking forward to the opportunity of fleeing to the comfortable security of America, but that is not to be at this time.

No, the powers that be have different plans for us. May I ask that you keep us in your thoughts and prayers as we continue to live out our lives here in the midst of this turmoil?

Your cousin, Q

He placed the letter in an envelope and then let Hilde know he was going to walk down and place it in the post. His mind was slowly adjusting to the reality of his future, and by the time he returned to their apartment, he had a new resolve.

His convictions to destroy the Nazi regime had weakened as he'd given over to the hope of leaving this fight to others, but now he found a new strength and resolve burning in his chest. *If it's my fate to stay here, then I will fight back however I can.*

"Hilde?" he called to her, watching as she came from the kitchen with a questioning look on her face.

"Q?"

"I've made a decision. I'm convinced that we're meant to stay here and do all in our power to destroy this regime from the inside."

Hilde nodded and joined him on the couch. "What's your plan?"

"How do you know I have a plan?"

She grinned. "You were out walking and thinking. When this happens, you always come back with a plan."

He put his arm around her shoulders and chuckled. "You know me too well, *Liebling*. I decided to take

Harro Schulze-Boysen's advice and start looking for work inside the government. The best way to gain intelligence about the regime is to be intimately connected to the regime."

Hilde frowned, and he tried to put her mind at ease. "I will be careful, but this is something I need to do. It's something I can do."

***

Several days later, Hilde received a letter from Zurich, Switzerland. She turned it in her hand to decipher the sender. *Adam Eppstein.* It took her a few moments to remember who that was. Her former boss and head of treasury at the insurance company. He'd been fired back in 1933 for being Jewish, and she hadn't heard from him since that day.

Esteemed Frau Quedlin,

I have to apologize for not writing earlier when we received notice of your matrimony. My wife and I have cut all ties to our former home country, but when we heard about the latest developments in Germany, I wanted to reach out to thank you.

I will never forget the day I was fired, and you were there for me, helping me to pack my things and giving me advice I didn't want to hear. You told me to take my family someplace else. Someplace safe.

It took me about one year to realize you were right. As much as I loved my home country, it had changed to the point where I couldn't raise my children there anymore.

In 1935, I finally found the courage to apply for a job in Switzerland. And after several months, the Zurich Kantonalbank offered me a position in their treasury department. My wife and I had difficulties adapting to the peculiar dialect they speak here, but our children now speak it like natives.

Leaving Germany has not been without its hardships. But every day we are thankful that we're here. The Swiss have been very good to us, and we have found many good friends.

The letter paused, the ink dripping as if Adam Eppstein had become lost in his thoughts for a moment. As the letter continued, the handwriting was shaky, and Hilde had difficulties deciphering the next sentences.

When we heard about the Kristallnacht, my wife had a nervous breakdown, so worried about her relatives, and mine, still living in Germany.

It took some time, but we eventually discovered that most of our male relatives were sent to labor camps.

My heart is torn as I write this letter. My family and I will always have you in our hearts and prayers. You truly were our guardian angel, and I believe without your assistance my life would have been forfeit many years ago.

I know things in Germany are getting worse, and I urge you to take all precautions and not to draw attention to yourself.

I hope someday in the future, we may meet again and I can thank you in person.

Your grateful friend,

Adam Eppstein

Hilde folded the letter carefully, tears streaming down her cheeks. Her hands were shaking violently. Her stomach rebelled as fear and emotion surged through her. She tossed the letter to the small table sitting near the couch and placed her hand over her mouth, fighting the urge to vomit. But a few moments later, she kneeled over the toilet and emptied the contents of her stomach.

She rinsed her mouth out afterwards and wiped her pale face down with a damp rag, then made her way to the bedroom on wobbly legs where she sank down on the edge of the mattress.

Chapter 17

Over the next few weeks, Hilde continued to get sick. Not wanting to worry Q, she managed to keep most of her sickness from him and was convinced that stress and anxiety were the cause of her sporadic illness.

Some mornings she would wake and throw up before she could even dress for the day. Other times, she'd feel fine, until her stomach suddenly rebelled at the smell of food.

That pattern continued until the end of June, where she vomited every single morning and then worsened. When she'd felt sick all day long, every day for five consecutive days, she made an appointment with the doctor for that afternoon.

Several hours later, she left the doctor's office, conflicting emotions raging through her body. At home she impatiently waited for Q, waiting to share the news.

"I had an appointment this afternoon," Hilde assailed him as soon as he opened the door.

"A new client?" Q asked.

"No...the meeting wasn't at work. I actually didn't go to work today."

Q looked up at her then. "You didn't go to work? Are you sick?"

Hilde shook her head, hiding the smile that wanted to break across her face. "I haven't been feeling well lately, and it seemed to get significantly worse this morning." She held up a hand when Q started to speak. "I'm okay. I went to the doctor. That was the appointment I spoke of."

"What was his diagnosis?" Q searched her eyes, and Hilde found she couldn't continue this small word game a moment longer.

She cupped his jaw. "His diagnosis...in six months, you're going to be a father." She watched his eyes go from concern to disbelief. He looked down at her still flat stomach, placing a hand there reverently as the reality of her words took shape in his mind.

"A baby? You're pregnant?" he asked in a hushed voice.

Hilde nodded. "I know the timing is bad–"

"Never! I'm going to be a father!" Q exclaimed, pulling her to her feet and dancing her around the living room. "This is the happiest news ever!"

Hilde laughed and giggled as he swung her around and then kissed her soundly.

"Stop!" she shouted, and as soon as he set her down on her feet she dashed to the bathroom.

Q came after her and held a washcloth for her. "I'm sorry. What did the doctor say about the way you've been feeling?"

Hilde cleaned herself and answered. "Morning sickness. The doctor said it may go away, but every pregnancy is different."

Several weeks later, the all-day sickness had receded to a mild morning sickness. Hilde was still able to work, but by the time she returned home each afternoon, she was exhausted and needed a nap.

After lengthy discussions, Q had convinced her not to travel to Italy, but to stay home for the summer. She was okay with that but needed some sort of break in her normal routine.

Q must have noticed her discontent. "Hilde, what if we invited your sisters to spend some time with us here during summer vacation?"

"I guess we could," Hilde said.

"You always have so much fun when you girls get together. Why don't you invite them to the city? You can take your vacation time and relax a bit."

Hilde smiled tiredly. "That's a good idea. Maybe if I could relax for a bit, this sickness would get better." She slipped down in the covers, then added, "But I don't want them to know I'm pregnant. We haven't told any of our family yet."

"That decision is up to you." Q kissed her on the nose and then wrapped his arm around her.

Hilde nodded, and the next morning called her parents to invite her sisters. Julia, unfortunately, couldn't visit because she'd been sent to a farm in Mecklenburg with the *Reichsarbeitsdienst*, a compulsory labor service for high school graduates. But Sophie was overjoyed with the invitation, and they made arrangements for her to travel as soon as the school year ended.

At work, Hilde informed her boss that she wanted to take her vacation time as planned after all, and he wished her a relaxing time off. Q helped her ready their apartment for her sister's arrival. When the day arrived, she met Sophie at the train station.

"You're here," Hilde said, hugging her sister tight for a long moment.

"I'm so excited! Thank you for inviting me. I was bored at home. Julia is gone, and Father says I'm too young to join the *Bund Deutscher Mädel*. Julia is only four years older than me." Sophie's eyes glinted.

Hilde smiled and looped her arm with her sister's. "Is that your only piece of luggage?" she asked, referring to the small suitcase her sister carried.

"Yes. I'm ready to go have some fun. And do some shopping."

Hilde smiled. "Lunch and then shopping." The two girls had a quick lunch of soup and a sandwich at a small restaurant. After lunch, they wandered through the shops and then made plans to visit a few museums and art galleries.

Over the next days, Hilde and Sophie moved about Berlin, shared laughter, and did all the fun things teenagers would do. Q had to work, but he joined them in the evenings and on weekends. It was almost as carefree as before Hitler came to power.

More than once, he told Hilde that he was so relieved to have Sophie around to take care of her. And just like that, her morning sickness abated. One day it stopped, and Hilde hadn't even noticed.

On Hilde's twenty-seventh birthday on August 23, Q surprised his two women with tickets to visit the open air musical *Der Mond* by Carl Orff. It was an opera-like production, based on the fairy tale *The Moon* by The Brothers Grimm.

After the last applause ebbed away, the three of them gathered their things to walk to Q's car.

Hilde looped her arm into her husband's and swooned over the beautiful music and the opulent stage designs. "Thank you, my love. This was such a wonderful birthday present."

Q couldn't answer because someone called out his name. "Wilhelm Quedlin!"

They stopped to see a man in a dark suit walking toward them. Hilde raised a brow at her husband, but he didn't seem in the least worried. Instead, he waved a greeting. "Erhard Tohmfor, I haven't seen you since we left the University."

"Yes, Q. Good to see you. How have you been?"

"I've been fine. Erhard, may I introduce you to my wife, Hilde, and her sister, Sophie."

"Ladies, it's a pleasure to make your acquaintance." Erhard Tohmfor kissed the hand of both women and explained, "Q and I go all the way back to first-semester chemistry."

"It's true," Q said, "but somehow we lost contact when we started our doctorates in different departments."

"I would love to catch up, but I don't want to take any more time from your evening out. Why don't we go to lunch one day next week?" Erhard suggested.

"Sounds fine with me. How about Monday at noon?" Q mentioned a restaurant near the shopping mall *Kaufhaus des Westens,* and Erhard smiled and promised to meet him there at noon. He bid his goodbyes and Q escorted the two women home.

Chapter 18

Monday arrived, and Q entered the restaurant to meet Erhard. The place offered a choice of three lunch specials and was crowded with people taking advantage of the offer. Q chose a goulash with boiled potatoes, Erhard ordered *Kassler* with sauerkraut. When the waitress delivered their meals, each one paid their share and Q inhaled deeply. "That smells delicious, doesn't it?"

Erhard already had his fork lifted, ready to dig in. "Yes. I bet it tastes even better. I'm hungry as a wolf."

"So, tell me what you're doing for work?" Q asked Erhard after taking a hearty bite.

Erhard chewed and swallowed a piece of *Kassler*, groaning in pleasure at the taste of the smoked pork chop before answering, "I'm working for Loewe Radio."

Q raised a brow. Loewe Radio produced all kinds of advanced radio equipment for the military, but they were also the manufacturer of the *Volksempfänger*, a small and affordable radio designed for everyone's use. He grinned at the memory of how he'd bought one of the first ones several years ago and *enhanced* it to receive short waves. The good old *Volksempfänger* still served him well, including listening to strictly forbidden foreign radio stations.

"Wow. You sure work for an *interesting* company."

"Yes. It's wonderful. I started there in 1934 and was just recently promoted to the manager of the chemical laboratory. We have the most advanced technology at our fingertips and enough money for research." Erhard beamed and went on to talk about their research in the field of radio engineering. "We're currently working to bring movies into the homes of the people with our *Einheits-Fernseh-Empfänger E1.*"

Q had heard about the E1, which was similar to the *Volksempfänger* radio, but with images. This modern device was also called television, and up until now, it had been prohibitively expensive for normal people.

"Congratulations," Q said. "Sounds like you enjoy your job." *Unlike me.* Apparently, Erhard didn't have to bother about budget cuts and diversion of research to military purposes.

"Yes, I do. There's so much going on right now. The E1 is for everyone, but apart from that, we're working on cutting-edge technology. Wireless transmission. Remote controls. Position tracking via sound waves.

It's a scientist's paradise." Erhard gestured with his hands and Q was transported back to their university days.

They'd shared the same communist ideals and dreams for the future. While the scientist part of his brain understood Erhard's enthusiasm for the new technology, the humanist part felt betrayed. "You've changed," Q said.

Erhard lifted an eyebrow. "How so?"

"You're working for the regime. That's a betrayal of what you used to believe in. Peace. Equality. Freedom. Everything your company does is geared towards war, even the E1!" Q had raised his voice and pushed his empty plate away.

Erhard gave him a sharp look and then looked around the restaurant. "Not here. Wait a few minutes and then follow me."

Q's jaw dropped when Erhard rose from the table and wandered down the hallway leading towards the kitchen. Curious, he waited the prescribed minutes before following the man he'd shared so many things in common with years earlier.

Erhard was waiting for him and pulled him out a rear door, into the alleyway behind the restaurant. He looked around. They were alone. "Are you still a *Gesinnungsfreund*?"

Q gave his friend a searching look. "Are you asking if I still share the same opinions as I did when we were in University?" When Erhard nodded, Q said. "Yes. My opinions haven't changed."

"Well, neither have mine." Erhard paused and then explained softly, "I thoroughly enjoyed the research work I'm able to do at Loewe. But when the company was Arianized last year, and the owners had to emigrate to America, I wanted to quit."

"So why didn't you?" Q asked, pressing his lips together.

"Because I was offered the position to oversee the entire chemical laboratories and the production process."

Q squinted his eyes and Erhard held up a hand. "Now, before you judge me, listen carefully. I took this position because it gives me the opportunity to work against the government by sabotaging the production of military equipment."

"What?" Q's brain needed a few moments to process Erhard's words. The man standing in front of him was doing the very thing Schulze-Boysen had suggested. Corrupting the regime from within.

Both men stood in silence until Q found his voice again. "I'm sorry I misjudged you, my friend."

"No harm done," Erhard answered. He looked around again before turning back to Q, searching his eyes for a while. He exhaled deeply before going on, "I could really use someone in the laboratory. A scientist, but also someone I can trust to do the right things."

When the door opened, and several employees stepped out into the alley, Erhard and Q turned and walked towards the street. They continued walking in silence for almost a block before Q looked at his friend and asked, "Can I sleep on it?"

Erhard nodded. "But don't wait too long because–"

His sentence was halted when two Gestapo officers stopped directly in their path. "Papers!" they demanded. Despite the August heat, they were dressed in long black leather coats and jackboots.

Erhard turned and saluted them with the *Hitlergruss*, Q following likewise, clenching his jaw. The Gestapo officers scrutinized his and Erhard's papers thoroughly before handing them back.

But instead of letting them go, the taller officer seemed to enjoy the change in his routine and started to ask question after question. "Where do you work?"

"Loewe. We produce radio equipment for the *Wehrmacht*," Erhard said and presented his employee badge.

"And you?" The other officer nodded at Q.

"I work for the Biological Reichs Institute," Q answered, handing over his own employee card. His neck hair stood on end at the prospect that these officers were bored and looking for trouble.

"Why are you two wandering around Berlin instead of working?" The officer with the soulless grey eyes asked.

His partner added, "Your behavior is very suspicious."

Q swallowed hard and glanced at Erhard, who didn't seem in the least intimidated by the Gestapo. Erhard lowered his voice conspiratorially and said, "You are very observant. My partner and I are on a secret mission, penned by the Führer himself, to find enemy radio senders."

Q blinked at the blatant lie, but Erhard even produced a simple voltmeter from his pocket and showed it to the officers. *A voltmeter? To find a radio sender? If those men have even a modicum of grey cells, they'll know this is bullshit.*

But the men were glued to Erhard's lips as he explained the operating mode of this advanced technical advice, sprinkling in just enough technical gibberish to keep them confused. Both officers tried their best to act as if they understood everything he was telling them and actually thanked Erhard for his important work.

Q silently laughed at the men's gullibility as they finally left, even saluting Erhard as if he were someone very important. He managed to hold his tongue until the officers were a fair distance away before turning to his friend with a nod and a smile. "Very well done, my friend."

"That was refreshing, wasn't it?" Erhard chuckled.

Before they said goodbye, Erhard held him back. "Be careful, my friend. There has been a huge surge in military contracts at Loewe in the last few months, and they all point to September. So far the war has been easy on us, but something much bigger is coming. Something the English and the French can't ignore."

Q nodded. "This I believe. Not because I have knowledge like you do, but it's a feeling in the air."

"One more reason to work for Loewe. You would be in a reserved profession. Protected somewhat even, as you've just seen."

"I need to speak to Hilde about this. I will be in touch, I promise."

Erhard gave him a hard look and then relaxed. "I understand. I look forward to hearing from you soon."

Q took his time returning home from work later that day. The conversation with Erhard weighed heavily on his mind, and he'd thought through things a thousand times. Now he needed to speak with Hilde.

As he entered the apartment, bursting with the urge to communicate, Hilde and Sophie were in the process of preparing dinner in the kitchen. He gritted his teeth and said hello. What followed was an endless chitter-chatter about their day as they ate, interrupted with a question here and there about his meeting with Erhard.

Q bit his tongue. This wasn't for teenage ears. After eating, he excused himself and retreated to his study. Pretending to work, he listened to the noises in the apartment until – finally – he heard the door of the guestroom close and steps approach his study.

Hilde peaked inside. "Sophie is asleep."

"Good." He all but jumped out of his chair.

"What's wrong with you?" Hilde asked, but Q shook his head and grabbed her hand. "Come for a walk with me."

Hilde grabbed an auburn cardigan from the hook by the door and pulled it over her short-sleeved summer blouse before following him outside. It was well after ten o'clock, and the moon was casting a dim light onto the deserted street. Q increased his pace, pulling her behind him until they came to a vacant bench.

"Sit," he told her but made no attempt to join her.

"Q, you're starting to worry me," she said and stood again. "You've been anxious since you came home."

"I want you to send Sophie home. Tomorrow."

She took a step backwards, her hand going to her throat. "What? Why? We're having so much fun together."

He pressed his lips together. "I need for you to trust me on this and send her home. First thing in the morning."

Hilde looked at her husband, crossed her arms over her chest, and shook her head. "Not unless you tell me why."

Q looked at her. "I don't want to have to explain myself..."

"Well, if you expect me to send my sister home tomorrow, you had better do so. I'm sick of your secretive behavior. You think I didn't notice your sneaking out at night, the hushed phone calls, the hidden papers in your study, and your growing agitation? I'm not stupid, you know?"

He sighed. "No, you're not." He wrapped her in his arms, kissing her hair. "I wanted to protect you. With you carrying our child and your sister here, I just wanted to give you a carefree summer."

Hilde leaned into his chest. "That's sweet of you, my love, but how can I be carefree if I sense your anxiety? Tell me what's wrong."

Q looked at her for several long moments before he pushed his breath out and said, "War is about to start."

"War?" She shook her head, looking confused. "We've been in one war or another since the annexation of Austria one and a half years ago."

"Yes. But something big is coming. A real war. Bad and ugly. My old friend Erhard Tohmfor confirmed my own suspicions today."

"When?" Hilde whispered.

"Very soon. Sophie needs to go home. Immediately. Please?"

Hilde nodded. "I'll take her to the train station first thing in the morning. There's a morning train to Hamburg..." Tears glistened, then spilled down her cheeks. "Oh, Q, it's really going to happen?" It broke his heart to see the fear in her eyes.

"I'm afraid so. Sophie will be much safer with her parents than she would be with us in the capital."

The next morning, they explained to a very disappointed Sophie that she had to cut her stay in Berlin short and return to Hamburg immediately. Hilde helped Sophie pack and Q drove them to the train station.

As Hilde waved goodbye to her sister, Q saw the tears stream down her cheeks. "We'll see her again," he assured his wife.

A few days later, on September 3, 1939, France and England declared war against Germany after Hitler's invasion of Poland two days earlier.

Chapter 19

By November, normal life had become a distant memory. In hindsight, Q could easily identify the cornerstones of the carefully planned attack on Poland. Just three days prior to that date, the German government had put into motion ration cards.

From then on, everything a person needed to survive – including food, textiles, and commodities – were being rationed. Each household, depending upon the number of people living there, was given a *Lebensmitelkarte*.

Q had to give the government credit for that. It was a clever move to handle the panic they knew would ensue as Germany entered into *total war*, and at the same time, it prevented hoarding of food.

As soon as Sophie left for Hamburg, Q told Hilde about the job offer from Erhard – and the subversive tasks coming with it. As always, she supported him in his fight against Hitler's regime, but he could tell that she still wished they'd gotten their green cards for America.

Armed with the employment contract from Loewe, Q entered the labor bureau and sat on one of the wooden benches in the long, empty hallway. A cleaning lady came along, mopping the floor until it sparkled.

In stark contrast to five years ago, the hallways were empty. The Nazis had achieved full employment of the German workforce. *But at what cost?* Q fisted his hands. This charade was ridiculous!

The door next to him opened, and a man with horn-rimmed glasses called him inside, gesturing for Q to take a seat after exchanging the obligatory Hitlergruss. The room was furnished with wooden desks, chairs, and cabinets that had seen better days. On the wall behind the desk hung a portrait of Hitler, flanked by two swastika flags. A shiver ran down Q's spine, and he grabbed his briefcase tighter.

"You're looking for a job?" the official asked with a friendly smile.

"No, sir. I came here to ask permission to quit my job at the Biological Reich Institute and–"

The smile disappeared. "Papers!"

Q retrieved the papers from his briefcase and handed them to the official, who studied them for a long time.

"Doctor Quedlin, your request is highly unusual. Why do you want to quit your current position at the Institute?"

"Sir, as you've seen from my papers, Loewe offered me a position to oversee research and development of radio technology–"

"Yes, I can see that," the middle-aged man snapped. "But if everyone in critical industries changed their positions whenever they wanted, we could never win the war."

Of course. Hard-boiled Nazi. "Sir, I understand your concern. The labor bureau has a much better knowledge about the needs of our Fatherland than the single worker. And I would never dream of quitting the job I have so wisely been assigned to. I came to you to gain clarity, whether the position at Loewe will allow me to make a better contribution to the war effort."

The smile returned to the official's face. "It's a rare occurrence for scientists like you to accept the superiority of knowledge of the labor bureau."

Q's eye twitched, but he forced a pleasant smile on his lips. "Thank you."

"Now explain how your new position is of use for the Führer and Fatherland." The official leaned back in his chair and folded his hands, watching Q attentively.

"The position I have been offered from Loewe would enable me to work directly on projects to benefit the *Wehrmacht* and ultimately the safety of our soldiers. Now that we are at war, this should be my first concern and the – albeit important – work in plant protection must take second priority."

The official leaned forward, enthusiasm in his voice. "The war will soon be over. Poland was conquered in four weeks. Next will be the French. They will be just as easy to defeat. And our Führer has plans for more."

Q didn't happen to agree but nodded nonetheless. "Aren't you worried about Stalin?"

"No, of course not. Our governments signed the non-aggression treaty and the Soviet Union has served us well dividing Poland."

Bile rose in Q's throat. The Soviet Union had been touted as an enemy of Germany for many years, and now suddenly they were best friends.

While Q was dealing with his emotions, the official put the required stamps on his employment contract and handed it back with a smile. "Do well for the regime, Doctor Quedlin."

"Thank you, sir." Q stuffed the papers into his briefcase and left the room, a sick feeling in his stomach.

Back at the Biological Reich Institute, he handed his approved written notice to the director, and a huge weight fell from his shoulders. At Loewe, he would be able to do something more meaningful.

Ever since Hilde had told him she was expecting their first child, an unexpected anxiety had taken hold of him. Money.

If something happened to him, he wanted to have the assurance that Hilde and the baby could live comfortably without his income. She'd grown used to a modest amount of luxury, and he didn't want her to have to skimp.

With that in mind, he had intensified his effort to sell the commercial rights to another one of his patents. Surprisingly, it wasn't all that hard because with the war in full mode, the companies lined up for the lucrative military contracts and some of his patents in the area of gas detection had become very sought after.

As he returned home, Hilde awaited him with a letter in hand. She looked even more beautiful now with her rounded belly, rosy cheeks, and shiny hair. Q kissed her mouth and her stomach, saying hello to mother and child, then took the letter from her.

Despite her protests, he retreated to his study to open it. He hesitated a few moments with a pounding heart before he meticulously slid open the envelope with the letter opener his mother had given him as a wedding gift.

Moments later, he stormed into the living room and stopped short in front of Hilde, carefully lifting her up and twirling her one circle.

Hilde giggled. "Good news?"

"Yes, *Liebling*. Drägerwerke agreed to buy another one of my patents for the modest sum of...drum rolls... twenty-five thousand Reichsmark."

"Twenty-five?" Hilde furrowed her brows and mentally calculated, "That's...wow! That's more than a five-year salary for you."

Q puffed out his chest. "I know. It's incredible, isn't it? I'll call your father to ask how to best invest the money. I want it to be there for you and the baby in case something happens to me."

Hilde's eyes clouded over. "Nothing will happen to you, my love. Don't jinx it."

"You're right," he said. "But I want this money to be our assets of last resort. With this war raging on, you never know."

After dinner, Hilde sat down to rest and knit a coat for the baby. Q retreated to his study and placed a phone call to his father-in-law.

They exchanged a few pleasantries and then Q cut to the chase. "Carl, may I ask you a question about taxes?"

"Sure. Although I'm more experienced in tax laws for companies and not for individuals."

"It seems I'll receive a modest sum of money for one of my patents."

Carl chuckled into the phone. "How modest exactly? Small amounts are tax exempt."

"Twenty-five thousand," Q said, and picked up the letter opener, rubbing the Amethyst stone with his thumb. According to his mother, Amethyst was his lucky stone.

"Congratulations–" Carl said, but Q cut him short.

"No, don't. Not before I actually hold the money in my hands."

Carl laughed. "Fine. With that amount, you have to pay the complete additional war tax of five percent. Apart from that, I don't think there are further tax implications."

Q shook his head. "I wonder what's coming next? On top of extra taxes and food ration cards, you must ask for permission to change your job, and getting a travel permit is next to impossible."

"Everyone says it'll soon be over," Carl said.

"That's what they want us to believe." Q rubbed the Amethyst again.

"So, how do you plan to use that money?" his father-in-law asked.

"Well, Hilde and I have discussed this. I think we should spend a small part of it buying high-quality things that will keep their value, even if we get another hyperinflation."

"Good idea. Like what?" Carl inquired.

"Jewelry and antique furniture were the two things that have come to our minds." Q grinned at the memory of the sparkle in Hilde's eyes at the mention of jewelry.

Carl exhaled loudly, and Q imagined him puffing out smoke. Carl probably had lit a cigarette as he settled in his chair to take the phone call. "Those are sound choices. You should also invest in gold coins. Now, mind you, you'll need to purchase them as secretly as possible and keep them hidden in a very safe place. I would suggest burying them somewhere."

"We don't have a garden, and I wouldn't want to bury them anyplace where someone else might find them. Or we could bury them in your garden? In case something happens to Hilde and me."

Carl raised his voice. "Enough of that depressing talk. Nothing will happen to you. Neither of you is a *Wehrmacht* soldier."

Q pressed his lips together. Even though the country was at war, most everyone pretended nothing had changed. *Maybe people needed this form of denial to cope with the danger?* "But people are worried. Some of my colleagues in Berlin spent their summer vacations and weekends helping out for free at the farms outside the city."

"Yes, same thing here in Hamburg. They want to secure connections if food becomes scarce," Carl said, sounding pensive. "I can still feel the hunger years after the Great War in my bones. That was an experience I don't want to repeat, and I sure don't want my girls to have to live through it."

"One more reason to invest our money safely. Thank you for your advice. Hilde and I will certainly treat this blessing carefully, should it come to fruition."

"Is there a chance it might not?" Carl asked.

"In these days and times, anything can happen."

"Well, I'll keep my fingers crossed. Are you still planning to come up for Christmas?"

"Yes. I need to buy train tickets because of the fuel rationing." Q grimaced and scribbled a note on a piece of paper.

"Let us know what day and time you will be arriving, and we'll meet you at the train station."

"We will. Thank you again. See you soon."

Chapter 20

Hilde shifted in her seat, trying to find a comfortable position. The train rattled through the countryside towards Hamburg. The fields were dusted with white frost and wafts of mist gave the landscape a mysterious appearance.

"I hope we'll get snow for Christmas like we did last year," she said and leaned against Q's shoulder.

"Statistically, Northern Germany has had a White Christmas every ten years over the past fifty years," Q answered, and she boxed him in the chest. He chuckled at her and glanced at her immense belly. "See the positive side. In your current state, you wouldn't want to shovel snow."

"No. But I would want to sit behind the window with a hot cup of tea, watching my husband do it." She giggled and then pressed a hand to the side of her stomach.

"What's wrong, *Liebling*?" Q asked with a worried tone.

"Nothing. Just the baby kicking me again." Hilde breathed and took the hand off of her belly to reveal a protruding bump the size of a baby foot dancing across it. "Look, it's moving."

Q chased the bump with his hand and chuckled.

"I hope it'll decide to be born sooner rather than later," Hilde said with a tired voice. In her last month of pregnancy, she felt like a walrus and every movement had become cumbersome.

Q's eyes took on a look of panic. "The baby isn't due for two more weeks. I told you it wasn't prudent to travel to Hamburg. What if you go into labor early? Here on the train?"

Hilde laughed away his concern. "We've discussed this at length already. The journey takes only a couple of hours. And the midwives in Hamburg are as good as the ones in Berlin should our pumpkin decide to arrive early."

At the train station in Hamburg, they exited the train, and her father met them on the platform. He gave Hilde a big hug and an appreciative glance. "My little daughter has grown up. And soon you'll be a mother yourself."

Her step-mother, Emma, had already prepared dinner for them. The next morning, everyone helped to decorate the tree for Christmas Eve. Mouth-blown glass bowls from the Ore Mountains. Hand-made straw stars in several forms and colors. As a finishing touch, Carl decorated the fir tree with real candles – used ones from last Christmas, but candles nonetheless.

Even though Hilde's half-sisters, Julia and Sophie, were much too old to believe in the Christ Child, the family still pretended it existed. It was one of the coveted traditions nobody wanted to give up.

But this year it was difficult to get into the spirit of the season. The war hovered over the country like a black shadow, ready to swoop down and wreak havoc. Emma collected everyone's ration cards, including the extra cards Hilde received because she was pregnant and managed to put together a veritable Christmas feast.

"Full fat milk! This is a gift from heaven," Emma exclaimed as she scrutinized Hilde's extra rations.

"That skim milk we mere mortals are allowed to buy is plain awful," Q said in agreement. "I'm convinced they've watered it down in addition to removing the fat and cream."

Emma smiled. "Q, would you go to the pantry and fetch me a bar of chocolate that I've hidden on the top shelf."

When he came back with the chocolate in hand, Hilde's mouth watered. It was so hard to get these little indulgences nowadays. But Emma took it from his hands and melted it in a double-boiler. Soon the smell of melted chocolate filled the house and one by one, every family member showed up in the kitchen.

Emma poured the full-fat milk into the melted chocolate and whipped up a delicious chocolate pudding for their dessert. Then she put it in the pantry to cool down, locked the door, and hid the key in the pocket of her apron. "This is for tonight. Now, everyone get ready for mass."

After church, Sophie jumped up and down. "Can we open gifts now?"

Everyone laughed and Carl chimed a tiny bell. The family gathered around the tree and opened their presents. Most of the gifts Hilde received were things for the unborn baby. Self-knitted onesies, diapers, a woolen blanket, and small boots to insulate tiny feet against the winter cold.

She thanked everyone before turning her attention to the large box Q had carried with them on the train. He'd been very secretive and had teased her about her curiosity.

"Open it, sister," Sophie urged enthusiastically.

Hilde smiled and pulled back the wrapping around the box. When she opened it, she gasped in delight.

Inside lay an expensive fur coat with a matching scarf and leather gloves.

"Let me help you try it on," Q said, setting the box on the floor and pulling her to her feet. He retrieved the coat from the box and helped her slide her arms in, but with her bulging belly, it wouldn't even come close to covering her.

Everyone laughed. "Your baby needs to come soon so you can enjoy your gift," Julia said with a grin.

Hilde kissed Q. "Thank you. It's so beautiful. And warm. I'll wear it as soon as our child is born."

The days wore on, and Hilde enjoyed the time with her sisters and – surprisingly – with Emma. The more time she spent with her step-mother, the more she came to like her.

***

Q enjoyed the downtime before he started work at Loewe in January 1940. He and Carl retreated frequently into the older man's study to smoke a cigar or cigarette and discuss politics.

Q said, "I don't buy into the official propaganda that the war will be over in no time at all."

"But the conquest of Poland went so smoothly. Maybe Hitler will stop at that," Carl argued.

"I doubt it. Not every country is going to fold like Poland did. And Hitler will only be satisfied when he's conquered all of Europe." *And more.*

Carl clenched his fist and raised it in the air. "I hate these damn Nazis! I feel so powerless. I wish there was something I could do."

For a short moment, Q was tempted, but he bit his tongue. It was too dangerous to tell his father-in-law the truth about his new job. The small measure of satisfaction Carl would get from knowing wasn't worth the risk of Q's secret getting out. He changed the subject, "How does Sophie like school this year?"

"She hates it. Since the war started, the quality of instruction has declined rapidly. Most of the young teachers were drafted, leaving only the ones nearing retirement."

"And Julia?" Q inquired.

Carl looked angry and then resigned. "She started *Reichsarbeitsdienst* this summer. She says she wasn't meant to become a farmer, but what can she or I do? She'll be there for a year...maybe the hard work will be good for her."

Q highly doubted that, but he held his tongue.

The discussion turned to their planned travel to America. "How did your cousin take the notice that you couldn't come to visit?" Carl asked.

"She was disappointed, as we were. But in hindsight, I can see that if we had journeyed to America to visit Fanny, we wouldn't have come back because of the war breaking out."

He and Hilde had discussed this fact many times. They would have lost all ability to communicate with their families – and to return home. "It seems the Gods had different plans for us."

Carl picked up the unexplained statement and asked, "Plans?"

Q glanced at his father-in-law but laughed it off. "Just a figure of speech, Carl."

Chapter 21

Hilde looked down at the baby in her arms with wonder in her eyes. She'd given birth to a bouncing baby boy several hours earlier, and like all mothers, she was filled with joy.

"What shall we name him?" she asked Q, who sat beside her on the bed. "We discussed several names, but I still like Volker."

Hilde smiled and nodded. "I like that name as well." She looked down at the tiny infant and ran a finger down his cheek. "Do you like that name, little one? Volker? It is yours."

The bell rang, and Q got up to open the door for the visitors. Hilde heard muffled voices and footsteps growing louder. Then a happy voice called from the doorway. "Knock, knock."

Hilde looked up to see her friends, Gertrud and Erika. "Come in and meet Volker."

Gertrud leaned over with her huge belly and hugged Hilde. "He's perfect," she said and added, "I'm so envious. I have another eight weeks to go."

"Time passes quickly. You'll see," Hilde assured her friend.

Then it was Erika's turn to hug the freshly-baked mum and her baby. "Congratulations. You're not going back to work anytime soon, are you?" she asked.

Hilde shook her head. "No, I don't want to go back to work for at least a year. I don't trust anyone to care for my pumpkin."

"Good. You need to have another child soon for the Führer. My husband and I are already planning on a third one."

Hilde shivered. *God help me if I produce children for the Führer.*

Erika had been completely taken in by the Nazis since she married a dashing young SS-Officer. Reiner Huber, son of the well-known SS-Obersturmbannführer Wolfgang Huber. Their wedding one year ago had made the gossip columns, and Hitler himself had sent his congratulations.

"You should have named him Adolf. That would have been an honorable name." Erika continued, and Hilde exchanged an eye roll with Gertrud. Erika's love for everything Nazi bordered on ridiculous. She even named her three-month-old twins Adolfine and Germania.

Hilde hid her face and turned her attention back to Volker while Erika continued to praise the regime. "Have you heard about the Führer's new plans to rid Germany of the inferior Jews and Eastern European races?"

Both Gertrud and Hilde groaned but didn't dare interrupt Erika's flow of words. Finally, Gertrud spoke up and reminded Erika that mother and son needed to rest.

When Q came back into the room, he saw the concern in her eyes. "What's wrong, *Liebling*?"

"Nothing. It's just...Erika. She used to be my best friend and now all she talks about is Nazi stuff. It saddens me."

Q sat down on the bed and fondled her cheek. "Don't feel guilty. You can't do anything to change her mind."

"I know." Hilde sighed. "But she drains my energy. I'd rather not see her again."

"Then don't," Q said.

If it was that easy.

A few days later, her mother and step-father visited. Annie showered her grandson with compliments. "Look how cute he is with his bright blue eyes and the light blond curls. He looks just like his father." Then she leaned over to take Volker in his arms, but stopped midway, holding the baby with both hands into the air, as if offering him to someone.

Annie's eyes took on a puzzled look in her struggle to figure out how to hold her newborn grandson.

"Mother, just hold him close. Support his head and don't squeeze him too tightly," Hilde suggested.

Annie attempted to follow Hilde's instructions but was confronted with another problem: baby drool. She desperately tried to hold him close while at the same time keeping his mouth turned away from her immaculate white blouse.

She gave up after a few tries and handed him back to Hilde. "You hold the baby. I can appreciate him better from over here."

Hilde bit her tongue as the almost forgotten pain of being abandoned by her mother came rushing back and compressed her chest. Now that she was a mother herself, the mere thought of giving her child to someone else stabbed her heart.

"Well, you should both get some rest," Annie said only a few minutes after her arrival. "We'll see you both later."

Later that day, when she told Q about her visitors, Q chuckled. "That's just like Annie. I guess she'll never change."

They were sitting together on the couch, Q's arm resting around her shoulders while Volker slept like an angel in his crib. Hilde sighed. "I wish Father and Emma could be here."

"I know. But Hamburg is too far to travel for a quick visit. Especially with all the travel restrictions in place. But we can send them pictures."

"Yes." Hilde snuggled up against him. "You know, I can now see how good of a person Emma is. She's done the best to be a mother to me, I just didn't want to accept it back then."

"Yes, Emma is a good person, and she's done a good job raising you," Q said, but Hilde had already dozed off in his arms. He carefully spread her out on the couch and covered her with a blanket.

She moved and murmured in her sleep, "I just wish my own mother was more like Emma."

Chapter 22

As winter gave way to spring, and the time approached for them to apply for a green card again, Q and Hilde decided to forego it. Their place was in Germany.

Q had begun working at Loewe as head of production. From the first day on, he and Erhard had weekly meetings every Monday to discuss "quality control" of production. Usually, they conducted this meeting in Erhard's office behind closed doors, but at times they had to inspect the production lines and the laboratories. At those times they talked in code.

Erhard would raise his eyebrows and mention that the defective goods rate was too high, and Q knew it was time to think of a way to raise it even further. If Erhard insisted he make sure certain spare parts arrived in time for a particular project, Q knew he was to delay the order and explain it away as a change in the technical requirements.

Soon enough, they ate lunch together and discussed all the world and his wife, but mostly politics. Q enjoyed those lunch breaks because Erhard was the only person – apart from his wife – with whom he could be candid. A refreshing change in an environment where he'd had to watch his every word for so many years and never voice his true opinions.

One day during their lunch break, Erhard said, "Q, we need more help."

"Why? It would be an added risk."

Erhard sighed. "The director called me into his office last night. He wants to promote me to his personal assistant starting next month."

"Congratulations," Q said with thinned lips, looking anything but pleased.

"I know, it's less than ideal because I will be tied up with administrative tasks and can't help much with our cause. But if I decline the offer, I will draw suspicion and might be of even less use."

"Then I'll do it alone," Q said.

Erhard shook his head. "No. You can't oversee everything on your own. And in many cases, you need a second signature for certain activities."

"I can still get your signature," Q stubbornly insisted. "Besides, we don't know whom we can trust. It would put our entire cause at risk."

"Dickhead," Erhard murmured.

"I heard that!" Q growled, and Erhard sent him a crooked smile.

"Let's give it a few more weeks and then discuss this again," Erhard suggested.

"Very well. I'll get these things taken care of." Q packed up his empty lunch box and left the room.

**

Later that week, Q and Hilde took baby Volker to Q's mother. At seventy-four years old, Ingrid had trouble walking and rarely left her apartment these days. But she loved Volker and the baby adored his grandma.

That night, she'd agreed to watch over the infant so Q and Hilde could go out with Q's friends to the movies. Hilde fussed over Volker, distressed over the idea of leaving him for even a couple of hours.

Q and his mother exchanged looks behind her back and Ingrid said, "Hilde, sweetheart, it may have been a while, but I raised four children."

"And she helped to raise my brother's four children as well," Q added.

Hilde reluctantly put Volker in Ingrid's arms. "I know, but it's the first time I've left him."

Ingrid skillfully tugged Volker to her chest and smiled at Hilde. "You two go out and have fun. Volker and I will do the same."

Q had already opened the door when Hilde turned again and gave Volker one last kiss on his head. "If he cries, he's hungry. I have put a bottle of milk in the kitchen, and it needs to be heated. But not too hot. You have to measure the temperature against the skin on your wrist—"

Ingrid laughed. "Sweetie, you go and have fun. Volker will be just fine with me." She cuddled his little hands. "Won't you, little pumpkin?"

"Can we go now?" Q asked his wife and escorted her out of the tiny apartment and down the stairs. "We have to hurry or the movie will already have started."

Leopold and his wife had already purchased their tickets and waited for them in the foyer.

"Here you are." Leopold waved them over. "You're late."

Q looked at Hilde and grinned. "She couldn't separate from Volker."

Dörthe laughed. "Ours are two and four already, but I remember those times." She put a hand on Hilde's arm. "In a few months, you'll be thrilled if you can leave him with his grandmother for some hours."

Hilde tried to put on a brave face, but everyone could see she was still worried about her son.

"Let's go inside," Leopold suggested.

As always, the theatre was packed. Nowadays, there wasn't much else to do for leisure. The popular movie *Wunschkonzert*, a love story with complications, had been Hilde's choice, but Q didn't mind.

Before the main movie was shown, they had to sit through several horrible propaganda films about the inferior race of the Jews.

"I'm sick and tired of being made to watch garbage like that," Leopold complained as he bought soda for Hilde and wine for the others during the break.

"Those short films would be hilarious if it wasn't so sad," Q added.

Hilde nodded and softly stated, "When I was taking Volker for a promenade in his pram today, I saw two women wearing a yellow star. They looked so...despaired. Beyond hope."

"All Jews must wear them now. It's to single them out," Leopold said with a firm nod of his head. "Has anyone heard from Jakob?"

Q and Hilde exchanged a sad glance and then Q explained, "Jakob was killed during *Kristallnacht.*"

"What? How did you find this out?" Leopold wanted to know, and Dörthe put a hand over her mouth.

"We were about to drive him to Hamburg Harbor. Instead, we found him dead at the bottom of the staircase of his parents' house..." Q swallowed hard, blinking back the tears. "If you had seen the destruction...it made me ashamed to call myself a German."

A few people passed behind them, and Leopold snapped at Q, "Watch your mouth!"

Q squinted his eyes at his friend. He thought Leopold was anti-Nazi. The bell rang, and they returned to their seats to watch the main film. As they prepared to bid each other goodnight after the movie, Leopold took him aside and said in a lowered voice, "There's a compulsory service coming up very soon. They need more soldiers for the *Wehrmacht.*"

Q nodded. Something was in the air because the military contracts at Loewe had risen to a new level. "Thanks for the warning. I'm working with Loewe in a reserved position for important military projects."

"And you enjoy your important work there?" Leopold asked, his eyes glaring daggers at Q.

"I do. It's very rewarding." Q opened his mouth to tell Leopold about his resistance work, or the fact that sabotaging military production was how he was able to enjoy his job so much. But then closed it again. He and Leopold went back to high school, and he had trusted him completely – until about an hour ago.

Even if Leopold approved of his actions – which Q still believed his friend did – the knowledge might compromise Leopold's safety. Or the safety of the employees at the paint factory he owned.

Chapter 23

As spring gave way to summer, baby Volker continued to grow, and each time Hilde looked at him, a surge of love rushed through her. But each time she looked at the baby, she also saw her two-year-old self.

The memory of how her own mother had left her at her grandmother's house stabbed her heart. Hilde caressed Volker's sleeping face – and saw herself screaming after her mother. "Don't leave me alone. Come back."

Nightmares had haunted her for years until she'd found tranquility in Q's love, but now everything came rushing back with full force. She breathed through the pain and blinked away some tears as the doorbell rang.

"Mother, what are you doing here?" Hilde asked, the words coming out raw. It was as if her very thoughts had summoned her mind's tormentor to her door.

Annie smiled and stepped inside. "I've come to see my grandson."

"He's taking a nap but should be waking up soon. Would you like a cup of ersatz coffee?"

Her mother grimaced. "*Muckefuck*? God, I have no idea how you can drink that stuff."

"Nobody likes it, but it's all you can get with the ration cards."

Annie nodded sagely. "I'll have tea then. Next time I will bring some real coffee for us."

Hilde could only wonder how on earth her mother sourced real coffee. Probably some high-ranking admirers of her famous husband who showed their gratitude with small perks.

She led her mother to the sitting room and went to the kitchen to make tea for them both. She carefully carried the tray back to her mother.

"Thank you for the tea," Annie said, taking a sip before leaning back and playing with her long pearl necklace.

"You're welcome. How are your husband and Klaus?"

"Fine. Although your brother might get drafted soon. He's almost twenty."

Both women paused and Hilde racked her brain for something she might tell her mother. The baby cried, but before Hilde was up, he stopped. "Why did you abandon me?" she blurted out before she could stop herself.

Annie was shocked speechless for a few moments. "What? You ask this now? That was a long time ago and should be forgotten by now."

Hilde shook her head. "I will never forget. It still haunts me."

Her mother blushed, her hand returning to the string of pearls hanging around her neck. "You don't understand. I was very young when you were born. I could barely take care of myself, and having the burden of an infant–"

"I was a burden?" Hilde asked, barely keeping herself together.

"Well, burden might not be the right word. Times were difficult because of the Great War, and I was all alone. I needed time for myself. I'm sure you can relate."

Hilde scowled at her mother. "No. I can't relate. You always put yourself first, even before your own daughter. You could have left me at grandma's for a weekend or even a few weeks or months, but forever?"

Annie grabbed her necklace tighter and rubbed the pearls between her fingers. "It was as much your father's fault as it was mine. Why didn't he take care of you?"

"Because he was a soldier at the front!" Hilde jumped up and paced around the couch table. "How on earth was he supposed to take care of me? Take me with him into the trenches?"

"Now you're exaggerating," her mother scolded. When Hilde didn't stop pacing, tears spilled from Annie's eyes. "If I could do it all over again, I would have found a way to keep you with me. Not a day goes by that I don't wish I could do things differently."

Hilde stopped, stupefied at the sudden change of her mother's tactic and stared at her. Even though she was sure Annie's remorse was fake, she couldn't help but sense a glimmer of hope. "You do?"

Annie nodded, wiping a few tears from her eyes. "I promise I will make it up to you."

"Mother, you don't have to make it up to me. Maybe we should just leave the past…in the past." Times were bad enough. Hilde didn't need to add to it by holding a grudge against her mother.

Annie got up and gave her daughter a small hug. It wasn't a grand gesture, but Hilde was choked up by the presence of something resembling an honest emotion in her mother's eyes.

Another cry from the baby drew both women toward the bedroom. Annie seemed intent on making things right and actually held Volker a few minutes, despite baby drool wetting her silky cardigan.

***

In the summer of 1940, Q and Hilde moved to a bigger apartment in Berlin Nikolassee. The two-story apartment building offered a big front lawn fringed by hedges and a smaller garden in the back accessible to all tenants that included a sandbox and a swing for the kids.

Hilde loved the new apartment and the surroundings. The quarter of Nikolassee was far enough from the city center to be as quiet and peaceful as Berlin could be. Within walking distance from their new home was a large green area with several lakes, including the huge Wannsee.

During summer, Hilde and Volker spent many afternoons at the beach of the lake, playing in the sand, splashing in the shallow water near the shore, and enjoying life. On some days, Hilde completely forgot about the war, but on other days, she was harshly reminded of the reality.

Today was such a day. Hilde and Gertrud had taken a stroll with the prams along the shore of Wannsee. Just before they reached the bridge to the island of Schwanenwerder, an affluent residential area, a bunch of SS-officers appeared out of nowhere, stopping the entire traffic – pedestrians, bicycles, and the sporadic automobile.

A black Mercedes limousine rolled across the bridge to one of the big mansions on the island. "Goebbels," Hilde said to her friend, "he's living on the island."

Gertrud pursed her lips. "I wish this war would soon be over. I'm worrying day by day about my husband."

Hilde nodded. The poor man hadn't even seen his three-month-old daughter yet. She put a hand on Gertrud's arm. "He'll come home. You'll see."

Her friend dabbed a few tears with her handkerchief, and as soon as the SS officers who'd blocked their way had disappeared, they continued their walk. Hilde kept her own worries to herself. Q hadn't been drafted because he worked in a reserved profession at Loewe. Nonetheless, she feared for his safety every single day.

"At least your husband is at home." Gertrud's voice broke into Hilde's thoughts.

"That's a small relief. I'm afraid he would refuse to join up because of his pacifist ideals." *And his hatred for*

Hitler. "And you know the punishment for desertion…"

Gertrud nodded. "Everything was so much better before the war."

Volker and Luisa, Gertrud's daughter, started crying jointly.

"Time to feed the lions," Hilde said, and they walked to the next bench to nurse their babies. As both of them suckled happily, Hilde continued, "My mother urges me to wean Volker, but it's next to impossible to buy full-fat milk, and how will an active toddler survive on skim milk?"

"I know. There's never enough quality food to be had with those darn ration cards. And I had to cut up one of my old aprons to sew a dress and a jacket for Luisa because I'd used all our textile rations for a new blanket."

"I know. Thankfully, Q is not very picky, and neither is his new boss, so I didn't have to buy a new suit for him and was able to use all the textile rations for Volker. I was also lucky that our neighbor handed me down a few things from her son."

Gertrud smiled. "How does Q like his new job?"

"He loves it." *Because he's one of the key players in a sabotage group and also gathering intelligence for the resistance.* "Erhard Tohmfor, his boss, is a friend from University, and they seem to get along very well."

"Have you met him?" Gertrud asked as she put Luisa back into her pram.

"Yes. He and his wife have visited us on a few occasions. Erhard is a wonderful person, a natural born leader. He brings out the best in every single one of his employees." Hilde sighed. She longed to voice her fears about Q's resistance work to someone, but even though Gertrud definitely wasn't a Nazi – unlike her former best friend Erika – that topic was off limits.

After she'd bid goodbye to Gertrud and Luisa, she pushed Volker's pram home and told him about all her worries and fears. He responded to her concerns with a happy smile and some sort of gibberish.

"You're a right slaphappy little fellow," she cooed to her son. "Don't worry. There's nothing we can do about it."

Since the birth of Volker, she and Q had steered clear of that topic. She didn't ask, and he didn't tell. But she had eyes in her head, and she noticed when he came home all agitated, or went out late at night, hiding papers under his jacket. He thought she was asleep, but she lay there awake, praying he would come back.

It was during those times when she would get up and go to the nursery to stand by Volker's crib and watch him sleep. Her heart full of love but heavy with fear.

**

The first half of 1940 was full of whirlwind military successes – Hitler's short succession of *Blitzkriege*. Hitler's Wehrmacht conquered Denmark, Norway, Belgium, Luxembourg, and the Netherlands.

Then, Hitler sent his troops through the dense forest into France, once thought impenetrable by the Allies. Much to everyone's surprise, the *Wehrmacht* marched into Paris in a campaign that lasted just six weeks.

Eight days later, Q came home in a foul mood. "I can't believe it." He took a closely guarded bottle of schnapps from the cupboard and poured himself a shot. "France surrendered. Do you have any idea what that means?"

Hilde didn't.

"That maniac is now dominating all of Europe together with his old crony Mussolini in Italy. With Franco's Spain and Stalin's Soviet Union friendly countries, there's not much left to occupy and subdue." He downed another shot. "Did you hear Hitler's speech on the radio?"

"No. I was out walking with Volker."

"Hitler called himself *Größter Feldherr aller Zeiten*," Q said. "Biggest general of all times!"

"He honestly compared himself to Napoleon?" Hilde asked, rolling her eyes.

Q nodded, his scowl growing deeper. "He did."

Hilde snuggled up against Q on the couch. "On the positive side, let's hope he ends the same way his megalomaniac idol did."

Q stared at Hilde. "What?"

"His empire collapsed, and he died exiled in Saint Helena."

"I know what happened to Napoleon," Q said. "But what makes you think that Hitler can be stopped? Who's left to stop him? The English?"

Hilde searched his eyes but found only defeat in them. "You can't give up faith. There are many brave persons like you and Erhard. Men and women who actively work to overthrow the Nazi regime. It may seem impossible now, but the night is darkest just before sunrise."

Q wrapped her in his arms and murmured, "That's why I love you so much. You never let me give up."

But the night had yet to become darker.

Hitler started a strategic bombing of England – the Blitz. In return, English bombers attacked German targets. Each time she saw or heard the planes flying overhead, she held her breath and prayed they would deliver their deadly load someplace else.

One day, they received notice from the government that every personal automobile had to be turned in for the war effort. Only doctors and food suppliers were exempt.

Hilde crumpled the piece of paper and threw it against the wall, but Q only laughed at her silent protest when he came home. "We never could get enough fuel to use it anyway."

She moped around for days at the loss of their means of transportation, until Q surprised her with two bicycles.

"Q, they are wonderful!" She smiled, incredibly pleased.

"Aren't they." He beamed. "Now we can spend our summer making excursions around the green parts of Berlin. Just imagine, we could take a biking tour around the Wannsee with the entire family. Maybe even sleep on one of the farms. It would be like a vacation."

Hilde's mood brightened at her husband's enthusiasm, "I would like that, but how do we transport Volker on our bikes."

"Oh." His face fell, and he furrowed his brows in thought. "Wait..." He left her standing and rushed off into his study room.

She shrugged. Some things would never change. Still smiling, she took Volker for a walk in his pram.

Q didn't mention the bicycles again, but a few days later, he brought home an old metal basket. The sturdy basket had a wire net around all sides, except for one. There it showed two holes in the net, the size of a big fist.

"What's this?" Hilde asked, eyeing that thing suspiciously.

"This is..." he paused, his grin growing bigger, "Volker's new bicycle seat." He pulled mother and son behind himself into the shed and attached the metal basket with pieces of scrap metal and wire to the front of the bicycle's handles. A few movements later, Volker leaned haphazardly against the edge of the basket, his feet placed through the holes in the net.

Hilde jumped to support her son. "Q. This is great, but don't you think he's still too small to sit in such a contraption?"

Volker snickered and explored the basket curiously.

"See. He likes it." Q beamed proudly. "Should we embark on our first tour?"

"No way. He can't even sit yet, much less keep his balance while we're riding the bike." She picked up Volker and sat him down on safe ground. "Thanks, Q. That is such a great idea, but our first tour will have to wait a few more weeks."

Chapter 24

Summer gave way to fall. Leaves started to change, and the temperatures began to drop. Q was having one of his weekly quality meetings with Erhard. The ongoing war had brought the company a surge of contracts, and Q had his hands full with overseeing and sabotaging the production lines. There was no time left for intelligence work.

"Erhard, we need to talk about enlisting some more help," Q said after he'd closed the door to the office.

Erhard raised his head. "Didn't you reject this very idea several months ago?"

"Yes. And I'm still convinced it's a risk, but with all the new contracts, I don't have any time to gather intelligence and keep in contact with our Russian friends. And…" Q scratched his head.

"And what?" his friend asked.

"If something should happen to me or you, we need another person to continue our work."

"Hmm." The seconds on the clock kept ticking away. Erhard rubbed his chin. "I actually have someone in mind."

"Who?"

"One of the head chemical engineers. Martin Stuhrmann."

Q raised a brow. "Stuhrmann? He's in the Party. How do you know he's on our side?"

Erhard took a moment to explain. "You've heard of Arvid and Mildred Harnack?" When Q nodded, Erhard continued, "They are old acquaintances of mine and part of a resistance group."

That was new to Q.

"Stuhrmann is a friend of a friend of Mildred Harnack. More than once, he's voiced his discontent with the Nazi ideology."

"Just because someone doesn't like the Nazis doesn't mean he's willing to work against them." Q shook his head. "We should test him before we tell him anything."

"Test him?" Erhard asked.

"Yes. We'll feel him out, then set a trap to see whether he's trustworthy or not. We'll take it from there." Q's head was already spinning, trying to come up with a plan.

"Fine."

In the following weeks, they started having their lunch with Martin Stuhrmann. He was in his early thirties, a solid and dutiful engineer who always triple-checked the requirements. His brown hair showed an accurate side parting and his hazel eyes carefully observed his environment.

Q and Erhard made a point to frequently discuss technical developments and politics, paying special attention to those technical innovations that benefited the military and the ethical implications.

After several weeks of doing this, they decided to set up a trap. Erhard called him to his office and closed the door. Martin seemed surprised that Q was also present, but didn't say a word.

Erhard started his attack. "Martin, I noticed the quality of production in your team has gone down again. Several times in the last few weeks, we had to throw away entire batches. And yesterday, the paste for the cathodes was contaminated and made unusable."

Q joined in. "When I ordered changes to the conveyor belt, the needed tool broke and stopped production for several hours."

When both men finished speaking, Martin was pale and trembling. He looked at Erhard with terror in his eyes and asked hoarsely, "Are you implying that I sabotaged the production line?"

Q and Erhard shared a look, then shook their heads in unison. "We're not pointing any fingers, but we do believe that someone might be intentionally causing these types of problems, thinking they might be helping to shorten the war and end Hitler's reign."

Martin's shoulders shivered. "No one would do that. Sabotage is a severe crime, and if caught, that person would be shot on the spot...or worse."

"Right." Nothing else was said, and they left poor Martin to figure out what had just been said.

Erhard then changed the subject. "So, when we have won the Total War, do you think life in Germany is still going to be worth living?"

Martin seemed confused. "Of course. I mean, isn't this what the government is telling us?"

Q added, "Or do you think it would be better for everyone if the war were to end now even if Germany wouldn't win?"

Both men watched Martin closely – this was the make or break test. What they had just asked him was very dangerous. If Martin were a Nazi, he would immediately tell the Betriebsobmann, the shop steward or talk directly to the Gestapo.

Martin watched them with big eyes and responded with a question of his own, "Are you implying that our Führer doesn't know what's best?"

Q and Erhard cocked their heads but remained silent for a minute. Finally, Erhard said, "Thank you, Martin. That's all for today."

Martin left the room scuffing his feet, and Q had to suppress a chuckle. "Poor guy. He's absolutely confused now."

Erhard agreed. "Yes. But his reaction will tell us where we stand. If he sings, it would be disappointing, but not life-threatening–"

"For us." Q completed the sentence. "Because you'll simply present evidence of Martin's sabotage acts to the Gestapo and they won't believe a word of what he said."

"Yes, and you will be my witness if that is needed. I already made a note in my journal that we suspect someone is sabotaging our production and that we've started interrogating people."

"But if he keeps quiet, we'll know he's on our side. Just how long should we wait?" Q asked.

"I think three weeks is a prudent time."

Martin told no one. The Betriebsobmann did show up in Erhard's office several times during the next two weeks, but it was always about routine work. One time, he reported on working accidents, another time to ask for time off for the employees to attend a Party rally, and so on.

It was a tense three weeks.

***

Erhard and Q had just finished another one of their "quality control" meetings when Q said, "I guess it's time to enlist our new helper."

"It is. But we won't tell him anything about our underground work – not yet."

Q nodded. He and Erhard understood each other. "Caution is the mother of wisdom."

"You're right, we can't be careful enough."

When Martin arrived, he looked slightly uneasy but took a chair at the round table in Erhard's office.

"Martin, you've done well since our last meeting. I need you to carry out an important task with the utmost discretion." Erhard said.

Martin's hazel eyes went wide. "Sure."

Q leaned back in his seat and observed the two men at the table with him. Erhard, his long-time friend and partner in crime, sat on his left. Nearly forty years old, his blond hair was cut almost military short and his piercing blue eyes seemed to be able to look right inside the head of those talking to him. His demeanor showed the signs of authority, while Martin, on the other hand, seemed to be sitting on hot coals.

For a moment, Q felt guilty about dragging Martin into their resistance activities.

"I need you to gather drawings, technical data and fabrication orders...everything one might need in order to start a serial fabrication outside of Loewe. Can you have this ready by the end of the day?"

It was an unusual request, but Erhard was the boss, so Martin didn't dare to oppose. He nodded.

After Martin left, Q raised his voice. "We should tell him the truth. He needs to have the chance to say no."

Erhard nodded. "And we will. Tonight."

***

The next day, the three met again for lunch. "How did it go yesterday?" Q asked them.

Martin grinned like a lightbulb. "Great. I wanted to give the papers to Erhard in his office, but he asked me to keep them until the evening. He told me he'd be waiting for me at the corner of Siemensstraße. I actually found this a bit strange and was somehow worried – but more curious."

Erhard chuckled. "Martin passed our test with flying colors, and I asked him if he wants to work for our cause."

Martin blushed at the praise. "You know, I was initially worried you'd accuse me of sabotaging the production, but when you mentioned the time after a total victory...I remembered our earlier discussions and noted there was a common denominator. I suspected you two were doing some kind of subversive work–"

"No such thing." Q stopped him. "We don't ever mention those words. You understand?"

"Yes."

Erhard added, "The less you know, the safer it is. For everyone. Don't ask. Just do."

Martin paused for a moment. Fear, anxiety, and pride fought for dominance in his eyes until he took a deep breath. "You're right. I know what happens to people who oppose our Führer."

"If the time is right, you'll get to know more. I have known you long enough to know you are on our side.

Now it's time to work until we've succeeded. One day we will harvest the fruits of our work."

"Well said, Erhard," Q commented on his friend's little speech.

The three men got up, and Q and Martin left the small canteen together. On the way to the laboratories, Martin barely contained his thrill. "When will we start? And how?"

"Slow down. I'll teach you our production lines and all the problems that could happen."

Two days later, during their lunch break, Erhard said, "Martin has solved his first task very well, now I have another one for you two."

Q saw the eagerness in Martin's face and chuckled. *Was I that enthusiastic ten years ago?* It seemed that, for Martin, their resistance activities were an exciting game, a challenging competition to outsmart the government.

Erhard's voice cut through his thoughts, "...I need you to make two short-wave transmitters."

Great. That would give them the opportunity to communicate with Moscow and possibly other countries. Q's mind leaped forward, trying to figure out where they could hide those transmitters. "We could disguise them as prototypes."

Both Martin and Erhard stared at him as if he'd lost his mind. "Disguise our employees as prototypes?"

"No. The transmitters. If we use one of the radio control boards the Wehrmacht has ordered and–"

"Q, Stop." Erhard cut him off. "I just told Martin that we need to screen all employees for reliability in case of an eventual upheaval. See why we need help? You'll take care of the transmitters while Martin oversees our employees."

Q scowled at his friend, but then he grinned. "Sure. I'll go and tinker with the equipment. Martin can talk to the others all he wants."

"Now let's go over the production goals for this week," Erhard said and fixated on Martin closely. "Always remember, our main goal is to increase production waste, but this must be handled carefully. It must always be due to a material defect, and never negligence of our personnel."

"If we raise the slightest suspicion that someone could be causing these problems, we'll all be in hot water," Q added.

Martin nodded.

In recent months, it had become more and more difficult to contact the Soviet agent. Thus, Q's focus had shifted from giving technical information to the Russians, to doing anything that opposed the German government. Sabotage, gathering important war information, and preparing for a life after this terror was over.

He still hoped that the German people would see Hitler for who he truly was and stop the charade. After an upheaval of the entire nation against their rulers, they'd need new, trustworthy people in place, and with Martin's help screening the personnel, Loewe would be prepared.

Chapter 25

As December arrived, Hilde and Q once again took the train to Hamburg to spend Christmas with her parents. It had been surprisingly easy to get the required travel permits. Not even the Nazi regime dared to interfere with German Christmas traditions, and visiting family was one of them.

Hilde leaned against the window and watched the landscapes pass by. Wherever she looked was destruction. The result of the continuous air raids. She sighed deeply and Q took her hand.

"I hope this war will end soon," she said. "It's getting worse every day."

"It will end," Q answered, "one way or another. Either we win the war and Hitler subdues all of Europe, or our country will be destroyed completely. The Allies will be even harsher than after the Great War if they win." Q shuddered.

"I was too young to remember the Great War," Hilde said and retreated into her thoughts while Volker was peacefully sleeping on Q's lap. She'd thought about returning to work next year, but Q had convinced her to stay at home with their son.

He'd handed her all the administrative tasks associated with his private research. Not that he invented much anymore. He was always afraid his inventions would be abused in the name of war.

But he still worked with a patent lawyer to sell the commercial rights connected to earlier inventions to other countries. Most of the technical stuff she didn't understand, but her typewriting skills came in handy with all the needed correspondence.

Sometimes he'd let her type up technical instructions regarding the radio production at Loewe. *He thinks I don't understand, but I do.* Her transcriptions would be given to the Russians either by Erhard or himself. She never asked, and he didn't tell, but she knew. She could see it in his eyes, in his posture, when the tasks he gave her belonged to his intelligence work.

She sighed again and looked at her sleeping son. Volker was a darling little boy with white-blond hair, bringing happiness to their lives without even trying. He'd inherited his father's curls and bright blue eyes, but her mouth and nose. *I'd give anything to see him grow up in a world of peace.*

"It's his first Christmas," she said, twirling one of his curls around her finger.

Q nodded. "And he'll celebrate his first birthday in less than three weeks."

"Do you think he understands what's going on in this world?" Her voice betrayed her fear.

"I doubt it. He's too young. But we'll make it as normal and harmonic as possible – for everyone."

"I feel a bit guilty that my parents haven't been able to see him sooner."

"It just wasn't possible to make the trip, neither for you nor for them."

"I know, but..." Volker stirred in his sleep but didn't open his eyes. They smiled at each other and stopped talking, not wanting to wake the tired child.

Some time later, the train stopped in Hamburg, and Emma met them at the train station. "Oh look. How cute you are, darling! You look even sweeter than on the pictures your Mommy sent me. Say hello to your *Oma.*"

Volker looked at her with bright eyes, apparently understanding every word, because he raised his little hand to touch Emma's face and babbled some incoherent sounds.

Hilde laughed. "He's intelligent."

"That's because he's my son," Q said with pride.

On their way to the Dremmer home, they witnessed the remains of the horrible air raid over Hamburg a month ago. Hilde involuntarily shivered. "Emma, we're so relieved nothing happened to you."

Emma stopped for a moment, and her lips tightened. "We were lucky, but many others weren't."

Changing the subject, Emma filled them in on the news of the family. "Julia won't come home for Christmas. She'll stay at the farm with the *Reichsarbeitsdienst.*" Her face softened, and her eyes glowed. "She's been offered a job in the administration of the farm."

"Aren't you worried about her being so far away?" Hilde asked.

"Worried? No. At least in the countryside, I know she's getting enough food. And it's safer. The bombers tend to concentrate on the big cities."

Hilde wanted to ask her step-mother why she wouldn't leave Hamburg and stay with Sophie in the countryside, but she already knew the answer. Just like herself, Emma wouldn't leave her husband alone.

For a moment, her heart filled with sadness because Ingrid couldn't be with them. Q adored his mother, but she was too old and fragile to make the journey to Hamburg. Instead, she spent the holidays with her other son, Gunther.

She grimaced. She and Gunther had never gotten along and had developed a pattern of avoiding each other, even after he'd moved back to Berlin with his family a few years ago.

"What are you thinking?" Q interrupted her thoughts.

"Nothing."

"Then why are you looking so worried?"

"It's just...I was thinking about your mother, and then Gunther. All of his sons, except for the youngest, have been sent to war. It must be so awful for Katrin and him."

"Since when are you fond of my brother?" he teased.

Hilde gave him a small smile. "Not of him, particularly, but I can understand the anxiety he must go through to have three of his sons at the front lines, waiting, hoping, and praying every day that they will come home."

Q squeezed her hand. "I know. Let's hope this war will end sooner rather than later, and his youngest will be spared the experience."

Emma interrupted them. "How old are your nephews?"

"Twenty-four, twenty, eighteen, and fourteen."

"Fourteen. One year younger than Sophie," Carl said.

"It's a crime against our youth! How can they be children in a world like this? How can they be happy and carefree when disaster is looming above their heads?" Q had raised his voice, and Hilde gave him a hug.

Everyone knew he was right. If the war continued, it was only a matter of time before teenagers like his nephew would be sent off to fight.

"Well, we won't let anyone ruin our Christmas holidays. No more talk of the war. Dinner is ready," Emma declared.

During dinner, they caught up on each other's lives. The company where Hilde's father did the taxes and handled the accounting department had changed and now exclusively produced war goods. Uniforms for the *Wehrmacht*, to be precise.

And just like that, they'd reverted to the topic of war. Emma shot her husband a sharp look and Hilde hurried to ask her sister, "Sophie, how is school going this year?"

Sophie made a face, "Awful. If there is school at all."

"I bet you do like the days without school," Q said, and Hilde thought she saw a mischievous light in his eyes. Despite his passion for science, he must have been a terrible student at school. She made a mental note to ask Ingrid about Q's school years.

"No. Those are even worse." Sophie pouted. "They make us work."

Q chuckled. "Well, I believe work isn't bad for you."

"This kind of work is," Sophie insisted. "For an entire week, we have to do our share in supporting the Reich. Like harvesting produce at the farms and orchards, or collecting old metal to produce more weapons."

Hilde swallowed hard. The Nazis used school children for war production?

Sophie had talked herself into a rage, and not even the stern glances of her mother could stop her flow of words. "I hate it! At school, they make us listen to the daily report of the Armed Forces, telling us about the great victories of our soldiers and then make us discuss the strategic masterstrokes of our Führer."

"Enough," Carl intervened. "I believe your mother wanted to hear nothing more about the war."

A long silence ensued until Volker rescued them with his cheerful nature and his need to play. He insisted on being put down on the floor, and everyone welcomed the distraction.

Volker had been pulling himself up on furniture for the last few weeks but had yet to trust his balance enough to let go and take his first steps. Now with a big audience, he clapped his tiny hands and then took two steps before plummeting to the ground.

Hilde jumped up with tears of pride in her eyes and hugged her son, praising him for his grand achievement.

Chapter 26

The next day was Christmas Eve.

Traditionally, they would decorate the tree together, but as Hilde looked around her parents' small home, no Christmas tree stood in front of the window. Trees were hard to come by and expensive. Instead, her father had gathered a few branches, tied them together, and affixed them to a wooden stand. It wasn't much, but it would have to do.

It took them all of five minutes to decorate the branches in a traditional fashion. A few of the precious glass bowls and some straw stars. Hilde was looking at the small manufactured version of a Christmas tree and could only shake her head. The Nazis had tried very hard to turn the Christian celebration into a profane festivity they called *Julfeier*.

Without much success though. If there was one thing the German people would argue about with their government, it was their beloved Christmas traditions. Not even the most die-hard Nazi supporters liked the idea of a *Julfeier*.

Hilde recalled a propaganda flier she and Q had found on the train to Hamburg. She'd forgotten about its existence and now pulled it out of her pocket.

"This is what is circulating out there," she said to Emma.

Emma gazed at the flier, then dropped it as if it were poison. "Over my dead body! We've used glass bowls and straw stars since I was a kid, and it will stay this way until I die."

Hilde picked the flier up and put it in the trash. The images of an SS officer hanging swastika ornaments on a Christmas tree made her stomach churn. *Nothing is holy anymore! Not even the birth of the Holy Child.*

When she returned to the living room, Emma was muttering under her breath and still livid. It would be funny if it weren't so sad. Like most Germans, Emma would never openly criticize the Nazis, but that was before they had attempted to mess with Christmas and the traditions she held dear to her heart.

Now she was acting like a lioness whose children were being threatened. Carl joined them, and upon hearing what had his wife so upset, he excused himself and returned with a leaflet of his own.

"These were being distributed at the company a few days ago."

Q took it and read it aloud while everyone laughed.

Reference: Discontinuation of this year's Christmas Holidays

Due to the circumstances caused by the war, this year Christmas will be discontinued.

Reason: The Holy Joseph has been drafted to the Wehrmacht.

The Blessed Virgin Mary has been mobilized as a munitions worker.

The Infant Jesus has been evacuated due to constant air raids.

The Magi didn't receive an entry permit.

The Star of Bethlehem had to be blacked out.

The Shepherds went into the trenches.

The Stable has been converted into a gun emplacement.

The Straw has been seized by the troops.

The Diapers of the Infant Jesus had to be delivered to the textile collection.

The Crib has been given to the National Socialist People's Welfare.

And because of the donkey alone, it doesn't make sense to celebrate Christmas.

As Q ended his recital, he glanced at the flyer and then at Carl. "They were handing these out at your company?"

Carl paled. "The company officials were already away for the holiday. When we came back from lunch, they were lying on our desks."

"Whoever made and distributed these leaflets, risked their lives for it. We need to burn it immediately," Q said.

"Q, aren't you over-reacting just a bit?" Emma questioned.

"No. Being in possession of this could land us all in jail."

Carl added, "Emma, he's right. I should have never taken the leaflet. By bringing it to our home, I've endangered us all."

Q stepped towards the sink and lit the leaflet on fire. When he could no longer hold it without singeing his fingers, he dropped it into the sink and then washed the ashes down the drain. Then he turned and looked at Hilde and the rest of her family.

How many more Christmases will be like this? Hilde wondered.

In the evening, after dinner, they opened the presents, which were rather modest and of avail this year. Warm winter gloves for Emma. Hand-knitted stockings for Sophie. Cigars for Carl. A sweater for Q, and a shawl for Hilde. The only person showered with gifts was little Volker.

Carl had gone all out and had overhauled the old wooden sled his daughters had used many years ago. At first, Volker was rather skeptical, but when his grandfather had taken him on his first trip around the house, he never wanted to separate from his sled again. After much yelling, his parents relented and put the sled beside his bed, where he could see and touch it.

Emma had collected all of their ration cards as soon as they'd arrived and gone shopping. The extra food rations given to all "true" Germans for Christmas had been a blessing, and on the 25th of December, Emma made a mouth-watering festive roast with baked potatoes and lard.

The entire home smelled of food and for once everyone forgot about the hardships of the war. Hilde helped her step-mother in the kitchen and watched with surprise as Emma took the finished roast and cut it in half. She carefully wrapped one portion together with baked potatoes and placed it into a brown paper package. In the end, she placed some cookies into a storage container and placed it on top of the meal.

"Hilde, would you like to take a walk with me?"

Curious as to what Emma was up to, she nodded and dressed Volker in his hat and coat before settling him into the pram. Emma placed the food package under the blanket at Volker's feet, and they took off for a walk.

They walked for quite a while before Emma veered them off the road to a small house. The shutters hung from their hinges, the windows broken and scantily replaced with wooden planks, the formerly nice gardens a picture of devastation. No smoke curled out of the chimney. The house had definitely seen better times, and according to the shameful state it was in, Hilde seriously doubted that anyone still lived there.

Images of the past stormed her head, and Hilde suddenly remembered. A Jewish family with three girls around the ages of Julia and Sophie had lived here for years. She swallowed back the picture of the neat and tidy girls playing in the garden while their mother lovingly attended to the vegetables and flowers.

"Are they still living here?" she whispered.

Emma gave her a meaningful look and a nod. "Yes." Then she took a quick glance around and disappeared with the package to the back door. Hilde heard a quick rapping on the door and Hilde felt a new level of admiration for her step-mother. Her own mother would never do anything selflessly without expecting something in exchange.

Several moments later, Emma hurried back to join Hilde and the baby. They returned home and had almost reached their street when Hilde asked, "Does father know?"

Emma nodded. "There's not much we can do, just tiny bits here and there." She paused and turned to look at Hilde. "I've come to the realization that this war is not good for our country."

"You are a good woman. I wish I had realized this twenty years ago. Mother."

Emma's eyes watered as she hugged Hilde tight. "This is the first time you called me 'Mother.'"

"I know," was all Hilde could whisper before she broke out in tears as well and the two women clung to each other until Volker made it known that he was tired of their walk.

Back at home, they found Sophie playing the flute while Carl and Q were absorbed in a political discussion about the consequences of this war.

When they entered Carl's study, his dark eyes flickered as he said, "To hell with all the home front talk. Goebbels can keep hammering the same idea into the minds of everyone. I don't buy any of it."

Q imitated Goebbels's voice and recited, "Everyone has to do their share to support the soldiers at the front."

Hilde laughed softly, "You could do the voice over for the propaganda movies."

Q shook his head and made a face at her. "Funny."

During the next days, Hilde learned just how much Emma cared for her family. Like most housewives who had the means, she'd been growing vegetables in a small garden behind their house.

She must have worked hard during the summer because the cellar was fully stocked with homegrown carrots, potatoes, onions, and a variety of other vegetables she had preserved in simple ways.

There were still winter vegetables out on the patches, including several heads of cabbage. From that, she had made her famous Sauerkraut by chopping up the vegetable and letting it stand in vinegar for at least fourteen days.

One day, Emma produced a special treat for the family from her secret storage. She made pancakes and topped them with homemade strawberry jam Julia had sent from the farm. With a shortage of sugar and sweets, the simple pancakes with jam were like heaven.

Every other day Emma would take a walk, hiding a brown bag with food beneath her coat.

Chapter 27

Q, Hilde, and Volker returned to Berlin in the first days of 1941 on a train ride fraught with adventure. Getting tickets had been difficult. With the absence of private vehicles and the increased rationing of petrol, the trains were overcrowded.

After the holidays, everyone needed to get back to work and even though private "leisure travel" was frowned upon, nobody had let Nazi ideology or war keep him or her from visiting far away relatives.

Q stored the pram together with their suitcases in the baggage coach and then followed Hilde and Volker to their wagon. They found a place crowded with several other people in a compartment. Q wasn't entirely happy. The continuous air raids over the capital and Hamburg were a constant threat, and he feared the train would be forced to stop.

To be safe, he'd taken a bag with enough food and drink for a day inside the train and crammed it onto his lap. He looked at Hilde, who looked beautiful and relaxed with sleepy white-blond Volker on her lap and her new flaming red shawl around her shoulders. A hidden worry nagged at him.

"How are we going to carry Volker if we have to rush from the train?" he asked her.

Hilde smiled. "Why should we have to rush?"

"If the air sirens go off and–"

"Q, there haven't been air raids in days. Why should the Allies start today?"

"Maybe because nobody expects it? Or because they're back from Christmas holidays just like we are?"

"You're overthinking this," she said, kissing the top of her son's head.

"Maybe I am." Reluctantly, he kept silent for a while, but then he looked at her again. "I'd really feel better if we were prepared. Just in case."

She sighed dramatically. "Since when are you such a pessimist?"

"Please."

"Fine. What do you want me to do? Tie him onto my back?"

It wasn't such a bad idea, but looking at her bright red shawl, he thought of a better one. "We'll use your shawl."

"Seriously?"

"Yes, stand up." He apologized to the other passengers and moved Hilde around, strapping little Volker to Hilde's chest. He wrapped her shawl around her body twice in a crisscross fashion before tying it in the back. Volker seemed to enjoy it, and Q grinned. "That will do. Now you won't have to hold him in your arms if we have to run."

Under the amused glances of the other passengers Hilde sat back down, trying to find a comfortable position. Not more than half an hour later, the abhorred sound of the air raid sirens screamed their warning. The train stopped, and the passengers were ordered to rush into a nearby forest to take refuge.

After three such interruptions, Q and his family finally arrived safely in Berlin, much later than they expected.

***

Several weeks after their return to Berlin, Q, Erhard, and Martin had another of their weekly meetings. Martin had become a very enthusiastic member of their small sabotage group and wanted to include even more people in their resistance effort.

"That's not a wise idea," Erhard replied with a shake of his head.

"But we could do so much more—"

Q jumped in. "Involving more people can only result in damage to our cause. And not just the cause, but to us and everyone involved. If we do too much, we'll attract suspicion."

Martin opened his mouth to argue his case, but Erhard cut him off, "Look, between the three of us, we have the entire production process under control. We don't need more people on the inside."

Martin finally nodded, and they moved on to other topics, including if and how they would keep contact with other resistance groups. After a heated discussion, they decided that only Erhard would connect with other groups while Q kept in touch directly with Moscow via the Russian agent.

"And what's my task?" Martin asked, disappointed like an eager schoolboy.

"You have our back in case something happens," Erhard said, but Martin didn't seem convinced. "Look, you're in the Party–"

Martin blushed. "I know, but I only joined because everyone did and it helped me to get promoted."

Erhard looked at him. "I'm not judging you, Martin, not at all."

"I will resign from the Party. I'll do it today," Martin said, agitated.

Q's jaw dropped. "That's a bad idea. Very bad."

Erhard nodded in agreement. "I concur with Q. People would start getting suspicious if you resigned from the Party right now. It would draw too much speculation on you, your family, and this company."

Martin's shoulders slumped, and he was a picture of misery.

Q sympathized with him. "Wait, being in the Party is a good disguise. You have access to Party meetings and can hear about things we never will. In fact, your task is to stay on friendly terms with the shop steward and keep an eye out for any signs that someone might suspect we're not working in the best interest of our Führer."

Martin beamed like a lightbulb with the assignment of this important task.

After he left, Q took Erhard aside and asked, "Aren't you afraid Martin might be too enthusiastic and give us away."

"No, on the contrary. I believe he understands our point and his new task will serve us well, you'll see."

Apart from sabotaging the war production and copying all of the classified technical documents to distribute them to their contacts, they'd started to prepare for the time after Hitler.

"We just have to open their eyes to how ridiculous and megalomaniac the war and Hitler actually are, then the German people will rise up in a revolution," Q said.

"Yes, but how can we make the leading managers of the company doubt the government without exposing ourselves?"

"I don't know yet, but we'll find a way. Have I told you about that satirical Christmas leaflet my father-in-law found at his workplace?"

Erhard chuckled. "Yes, it actually was quite funny."

"So there are like-minded people who won't keep quiet anymore. Not that I think leaflets are enough to overthrow Hitler, but they are a start to make people think – and doubt."

***

A week later, Q was sitting at his desk, deep in concentration. He was copying top-secret material to make a blueprint for a serial production of radio equipment somewhere else when Martin walked into the laboratory.

Q looked up and frowned at him. Martin of all persons should know he didn't appreciate interruptions when he was deep in thought. But instead of retreating, the intolerable fool stepped forward, not paying attention to where his feet walked. He tripped, spilling a full mug of ersatz coffee all over the papers in front of Q.

Q jumped up, opening his mouth to angrily reprimand the young man when he became aware of the two *Luftwaffe* officials, two men in Gestapo uniforms, and the shop steward right behind Martin.

He swallowed hard and busied himself with removing the sodden papers and wiping up his workspace while the shop steward shot Martin a sharp glance. "Can't you take better care, Stuhrmann?"

Martin made his best effort to look contrite. "I'm so sorry." But the shop steward had already gestured for him to shut up and addressed the officials, "*Meine Herren,* please rest assured that no liquid is allowed in the production hall. Our workers have to go to the break room for any refreshments. Unfortunately, scientists insist they get special treatment."

The *Luftwaffe* major seemed to be in a good mood because he only nodded. "Yes. Yes. Now let's continue with our inspection."

The shop steward clicked heels and said, "Major Schmid, please follow me to where we produce the state-of-the-art radio equipment for our armed forces. Our head of production, Martin Stuhrmann, will answer all your questions."

Q glanced at Martin and nodded a silent *thank you* before the group crossed the laboratory and walked through the door to the production hall. Q returned to his work with trembling hands.

That evening, when Q headed home, he was still shaking from the encounter.

Dinner was cold – again.

Chapter 28

"I'm sorry, my love. I couldn't get enough coal to heat the oven in the kitchen. The little I got I used to heat the living room," Hilde said.

"I don't care."

She looked at him and frowned. "What's wrong with you, my love? Did you have a bad day?"

Q merely nodded. "I'll tell you when the baby is asleep."

Two hours later, they sat together on the couch and she snuggled up to him while he told her everything that had happened.

"It sounds like Martin proved himself today, if you still had any doubts about him."

He kept quiet for a while, stroking her arm. "I don't know how much longer I can do this."

"You need to stay strong and continue. I'm afraid all the time, and there will always be times when we want to give in to our fear, but I know you – you need to stand up for what you believe in."

"But at what cost?" Q asked her.

"What if everyone just gave in? There would never be an end to this. Our country needs people like you."

His voice was tired when he answered, "I'm not sure our country is worth the effort anymore."

Hilde ran her hand through his curls. "Then do it for our son. For his future, so he can grow up in a country worth living. Be a good role model for him."

Q turned his head and kissed her. "I admire you. You are so strong, and you make me want to be a better man. You're the best life companion I could ever have wished for." They kissed again, and he promised, "One day, when this war is over, we'll enjoy our lives again. Just like during our honeymoon. Only better."

Hilde snuggled close in his arms. "I hope that day comes sooner rather than later."

She heard the air raid sirens in the distance, just like almost every night. Both of them held their breath, ready to get Volker from his crib and rush into the cellar of the building that served as a bomb shelter, but the sirens faded away.

Hilde sighed. "I'm so thankful we moved out here. If we still lived in the center, we'd have to spend almost every night in the shelter."

"Yes, it was a good decision, for several reasons. There's not much out here worth bombing, only lakes and greens."

"Yes." Hilde shivered in his arms, and he asked, "Are you cold, *Liebling*?"

"No, I believe I haven't told you. Last week when Volker and I visited your mother, we passed in front of our old apartment building." Her voice broke. "It was bombed out and completely uninhabitable. Oh my God! Will this nightmare ever end?"

***

The next day, Q went back to work with a fresh sense of purpose and renewed courage. They'd just received a huge order to deliver a new and enhanced portable transmitter to the *Wehrmacht* by June.

The urgency in the date of delivery made Q wonder which country Hitler wanted to attack next. He and Erhard discussed the possibilities, and as the list of countries not already under Nazi control wasn't very long, they came to the conclusion it must be England.

Just how to warn them? They didn't have contacts within the English government.

Q sighed in desperation, and instead, they worked on a plan to delay production of the portable transmitters. Q got right to work and accidentally destroyed an important tool needed to make the prototype. Unfortunately, it was the only one Loewe had, and he walked into the director's office, head bowed and shoulders dropped.

Shifting from one foot to another, he started his apology. "Sir, I'm so sorry, but when I tested the radio frequencies of the prototype for the *Wehrmacht*, our measuring device blew up."

The director scolded him about his imprudence and raised his voice loud enough to attract Erhard Tohmfor into his office. "Sir, is there a problem?"

When Erhard became aware of Q staring guiltily at the floor, he could hardly hide a smile and looked in the other direction.

"Yes. Doctor Quedlin has ruined some measuring device that is needed for the new prototype!" the director shouted.

As always, Erhard had the situation under control and answered calmly, "Director, I agree this is rather unfortunate. I have mentioned time and again that we need backup tools in case such a thing happens. Unfortunately – as you know – it is almost impossible to source anything non-essential. The government seems to believe that our tools don't have a shelf-life, but they do. Most of our tools are way too old to work reliably."

Now it was Q's turn to stare at his toes to hide a grin. While Erhard was right on the general condition of their equipment, this particular tool could have served for another thirty years, if he hadn't crossed two wires before using it, thus effectively ruining the measuring device. It had been a nice little explosion.

In his early days as a scientist, he'd always been afraid to ruin something and been overly careful, but now he felt an immense adrenaline rush whenever something went wrong.

The director spoke again. "Fine. Order a new one. Make it urgent."

Erhard nodded, and Q left the office, putting on his most contrite face. Back at the lab, he gave Martin a silent thumbs up when he told him about the ruined device.

Martin nodded and explained, "We also have a problem with the fabrication machines for the casing. They started failing, and it took me an entire day to find the cause."

"I hope you were able to fix it." Q smirked.

"Unfortunately not. The motors have seized up due to bad quality transmission oil. It had too much particulate material in it, and I had to throw everything away. We need to wait for the next batch to arrive."

Particulate material as in sand and metals shards you poured into the oil? "It's so hard to buy high-quality raw materials. I wonder what is next?"

For Q and Martin, it was like a game, trying to outdo each other in wreaking the most havoc on production progress. Sometimes Erhard had to slow them down and caution them to be more subtle in their sabotage work.

***

Summer arrived, and Q finally received the answer as to where Hitler had his sights set next.

The Soviet Union.

Erhard and his wife were visiting Hilde and Q the night the news broke that Hitler's troops had mounted an attack against the Soviet Union because Stalin had been plotting against Germany.

Hilde raised her hand to her mouth. "Weren't our two countries supposed to be allies?"

"Well, apparently not anymore," Q responded.

"I can't believe Hitler attacked his friend Stalin and mounted the largest offensive so far in this war," Erhard said.

His wife shook her head, the shock still lingering in her eyes. "Obviously, the accusation about plotting against our country must be fabricated."

Q's hands curled into tight fists. "We must increase our efforts. If Hitler wins this war against Russia, his next goal is the entire world."

The next day, the Russian agent contacted Q. He'd relayed intelligence to Pavel for several years now and almost considered him a friend.

Pavel didn't have good news for him. "I'm leaving for Moscow today, and we won't be able to meet again. I can't tell you if and how you'll be contacted from now on. As I speak, all agents are recalled home."

"I wish you well and have a safe trip home." Q swallowed. "Tell your leaders that we are at your disposal for anything needed to shorten this war. Neither my helpers nor I have changed opinions."

The agent produced a map, which he tore into two halves and gave one part to Q, "If another agent contacts you, ask him for the other half of that map. If he can't produce it, he's not on your side."

"What about asking if the hike up Mount Etna is strenuous?"

"Who told you that?" Pavel asked confused.

"The other agent, the one I met in Sicily."

"Oh." Pavel's eyes clouded. "I didn't know about that. Well then, to be on the safe side, ask for both."

Chapter 29

On a hot summer day in August 1941, Hilde met with Gertrud and Erika and a bunch of kids at the Wannsee beach. It was the favorite gathering for mothers with small children, a getaway within the city limits to forget the sorrows of war, even if only for a few hours.

Despite Hilde's intentions not to see her former friend and converted Nazi anymore, Q had encouraged her to reconnect with Erika. Her father-in-law was SS Obersturmbannführer Wolfgang Huber, and Hilde might be able to gather some valuable information she could pass along to Q.

Like always, Erika was singing the praises of Hitler, and Hilde did her best to swallow down the bile forming in her throat. She wanted to punch some common sense into that woman. Did she even understand what garbage she was regurgitating?

Thankfully, Gertrud steered the conversation to safer topics. Children. Erika had just given birth to her first boy three months earlier. She raved about the baby's Aryan looks, his blond hair, and his tall frame.

Hilde bit back a sharp remark. The boy looked like any baby, with little to no hair, and not especially tall or strong. On the contrary, he was cute and chubby.

After a while, Gertrud said, "Hilde, I envy you."

"Me? Why?" Hilde wanted to know.

"You still have your husband around. Mine has been transferred to the Eastern Front. We just saw him for a few days of leave of absence."

Gratitude spread across Hilde's body even as she felt sorry for her friend. Q's resistance work was dangerous, but maybe not as dangerous as the front. "Yes, I'm so grateful he's working in a reserved profession."

Erika chimed in, "Q is doing valuable work, but my husband is following in the footsteps of his father and has recently been promoted. He's in Paris." Her eyes became dreamy. "He wrote me that I should be able to visit soon, when little Adolf is a bit older and can stay with my mother."

Hilde shivered, she still couldn't wrap her mind around the fact that Erika had named her children Adolfine, Germania, and Adolf. *Disgusting!*

She tucked that thought away and turned her attention to the children. Volker was now a year and a half old and was walking around like a pro. He was an active little boy but lately had been having problems with his digestion.

"Volker has been sick again this week. He's thrown up two nights in a row, and I'm seriously worried. If I could only get some healthy food for him, and not the crap we can buy with the ration cards."

Erika sent her a scolding glance. "Hilde, everyone has to make sacrifices for the war. You shouldn't be complaining."

Hilde hid her hurt at this reaction and soon found an excuse to leave. Q might find it valuable to stay in touch with Erika, but she couldn't stomach her former friend's Nazi talk one minute longer.

Several days later, Q came home, tired as usual. The constant anxiety and the secrecy were taking a toll on him, and Hilde thought about something to cheer him up. She'd been keeping a sweet secret from him, waiting for the right moment.

Now as he complained once again about the futility of his sabotage efforts, she decided this would be as good a moment as any other. "Q, you must carry on. You need to be a good role model for your children."

Q started to respond but then her last word gave him pause. "Children? As in, more than one?" He looked at her, and she saw the happy smile on his face.

"Yes, I'm pregnant again."

Q grabbed her and spun her around the room. "I'm so happy, and I love you so much."

But as slaphappy as they both were, Hilde was also worried. They were in the middle of the worst war of all time, and they were going to bring another child into the world?

He sensed her unease and assured her, "*Kommt Zeit, Kommt Rat!*" Time will tell.

Chapter 30

Q needed Hilde out of the house. And not because she was pregnant. He needed to think what else he could do. Dangerous things.

He'd never been able to hide something from Hilde, and she would only worry if she found out.

When yet another broadcast praised the virtues of the *Kinderlandverschickung* – the evacuation of children from the big cities into the countryside – he raised the topic with Hilde.

"No way! I will not leave Volker in the hands of some Nazi nurses," she growled.

That was a point for her. Volker would soon turn two years old and was too young to understand, but he wouldn't want him indoctrinated with their ideology. "So why don't you go with him?" he suggested, trying to sound casual.

"And suffer their indoctrination day in day out? It's bad enough to hear Erika singing Hitler's praise, I don't need to listen to a bunch of overenthusiastic nursery teachers."

"Maybe you could go and stay at your parents' place for a while?"

She scoffed. "Hamburg is as much a target of the bombings as Berlin. In fact, it's worse for them. We've only had the occasional air raids."

Q sighed. This wasn't going the way he wanted it to. "What about Julia? She's on a farm near Magdeburg, and that's only a few hours train ride from Berlin. You could take Volker there. It might even help with his digestion problems."

"I don't want to leave you here alone. Who knows if I'll ever see you again?"

"*Liebling*, nothing will happen to me. But you're six months pregnant, and you need to rest. Face it, Berlin isn't safe anymore. You aren't getting enough sleep because of the air raids. Things need to change."

Hilde nodded. He was right. Even though their quarter hadn't taken a hit, not a day or night went by where they weren't forced to leave their beds and seek shelter. It was wearing her down both physically and mentally.

"Q, I don't want to leave you–"

"It won't be forever, but you need a break. Please take Volker and stay with Julia for a while. I'll join you for Christmas. That's only a few weeks away."

Hilde finally agreed. Normally, it was almost impossible to obtain a travel permit for personal or leisure travel. But because Hilde was pregnant and had a small child with her, she made a convincing case that she had to leave Berlin for a while and she received her travel papers without any problems.

Two days before she travelled, she came home livid and recounted what had happened as she stood in line waiting for her turn to get the travel permit stamped.

"You won't believe this, Q! That official saw that I was pregnant and congratulated me."

"Well, that isn't a reason to be angry, or is it?"

"Yes, it is. His exact words were, 'Congratulations for giving our Führer yet another Aryan child.'"

Q put his hands on her shoulders to calm her down, but couldn't stop himself from laughing out loud. "I hope you didn't punch him in the face."

She scowled at him but then joined his laughter. "I wanted to, but the urge to vomit on his shoes was bigger."

"You didn't...?"

"No, I didn't. I managed to get hold of a waste paper basket. You can't imagine how fast my papers were stamped and finished."

On the morning of December 6th, he took her and Volker to the train and sent them off to Magdeburg.

Chapter 31

The next day, Q met with his old friends Leopold and Otto. It always gave him a stab to the heart because they'd always been a quartet – until Jakob was murdered in the *Kristallnacht*.

So many things had happened since then, most of them bad. The friends had a silent understanding not to talk about politics, but today was different. As they sat in the bar, the usual music broadcast was interrupted by an urgent message and someone raised the volume on the radio.

"We interrupt this program to bring you a special message. Our esteemed ally, Japan, has successfully beaten the United States of America. In a surprise attack, Japanese bombers attacked the Naval Station located in Oahu, Hawaii, crippling and destroying both their mediocre Navy and Air Force. Even now, Pearl Harbor burns and Germany celebrates our ally's victory.

"The Führer is very optimistic that the war will soon be won, and Germany will prevail over her enemies. The spiteful United States of America has paid for its interference, and other nations will soon reap their just rewards at the hands of German soldiers."

Turmoil ensued in the bar, everyone talking at once. Most of the guests – all of them in uniform except for the three friends – echoed the opinions of the radio speaker, but Q thought differently. *Thank God. Now America will have to officially enter the war.* "It's over. Germany is going to lose this war."

"I wouldn't be so sure. Hitler won't be stopped," Otto responded.

Q had yet to figure out on which side Otto stood. He'd not joined up but pulled a few strings to have his research work at the University be classified as *reserved profession.*

The same was true for Leopold. He owned a paint factory and seemed to be unbothered by the Nazis. While Q trusted Leopold completely on a personal level, he didn't necessarily trust his political convictions. It would be wiser to keep quiet.

"You're probably right," he said and changed the topic. "Have you been able to crack down the hydrogen cyanide molecules, Otto?"

Otto nodded. "We're working on it. It's highly poisonous and extremely flammable." Q exhaled in relief as the subject was safely navigated into a direction they all were comfortable with.

When they bid their goodbyes, Q was convinced that he needed to do more. Much more. Sabotage and intelligence gathering wasn't enough. He wanted to do something bold, something that would forever change the course of history. But what?

As he walked to the tram station with Leopold, they could see the red lights of the airport Tempelhof in the distance. Suddenly, Q had an idea. He sent Leopold off on the tram and opted to walk home. It would take him three or four hours, plenty of alone time to think through his new idea.

The next day, he stormed into Erhard's office. "I have a brilliant idea!"

"Care to share it with me?" His friend chuckled.

"That's why I'm here. Let's take a walk, and I'll explain it to you."

"A walk? It's nine o'clock. I have work to do." But as he looked into Q's excited face, he took his hat and coat and left his office. On the way out he advised the secretary, "Fräulein Golz, Doctor Quedlin and I have an urgent appointment to visit with one of our suppliers. We'll be back in about an hour."

As soon as they'd left the company grounds and were out of earshot of anyone, Q started to explain. "I thought we could produce remote controlled blinkers."

"Blinkers, what for?" Erhard asked.

"That's the good part. With the remote control, we can make them start blinking when hostile aircraft is incoming and–"

"But how would we know when hostile aircraft was coming?"

Q thought for a moment. "Just like anyone else. Via the air raid sirens."

"Fine. And where do we position those blinkers and why?"

"We'll install them on the roofs of military buildings. When they start blinking, the English pilots can easily spot the strategic buildings to bomb and avoid civilian targets."

"Hmm." Erhard stopped walking. "It is a brilliant idea. And it could save thousands of civilian lives."

Q grinned. "Yes, it's fantastic, and we have all the means to do it. We can use one of the production lines on the weekends to make the blinkers, and we can easily build two or three remote controls as well."

"But we would need to be near the buildings because the range of the remote controls isn't very far," Erhard objected. "We could only light two or three buildings at the same time, and how fast can we get there once we hear the sirens? From where you live, it'll take much too long to get to any strategic military building."

"I haven't thought about that." Q shook his head and took up the walking again. "What if we use the short wave radio transmitters we're building for the Wehrmacht? I'm sure I can come up with a way to alter the blinkers so they could receive the radio signal. This way we can light all the buildings from wherever we are."

Erhard nodded. "Yes, we just have to keep the transmitter with us at all times."

"We should let Martin in on the plan," Q said. With new hope and a sense of accomplishment, they returned to the factory, but right before they reached the grounds, Erhard asked, "Just how do we get those blinkers onto the buildings? It's not like we can simply go up there and assemble them."

Chapter 32

Hilde shared the train compartment with a young woman who looked exceptionally dirty and unkempt. Like someone who'd just crawled out of a heap of rubble. She couldn't hold back her curiosity and started a conversation with the girl who introduced herself as Annegret.

Annegret confirmed her fear, telling her that she had been bombed out that day.

"Oh, I'm so sorry. That must have been an awful shock," Hilde said with genuine empathy, but before she could ask more details, the ticket officer entered and Hilde presented her papers.

Just as the man wanted to return her papers, a Gestapo officer entered their compartment. Even though Hilde's papers were in order, she still felt shivers running down her spine. The picture of SS men beating a handbag thief to death was too deeply ingrained in her brain. As was the ever-present fear that they'd uncovered Q's resistance work and came to arrest her.

She waited with bated breath and tried not to show her relief when he finally returned her papers and turned his attention to Annegret. "Papers?"

The young woman suddenly looked like a frightened rabbit. *Well, doesn't every normal citizen hold their breath in the presence of Gestapo or SS?*

The stern expression of the Gestapo officer softened as he read out loud Annegret's name and repeated it before he came to attention. "Fräulein Huber, may I say how sorry I am for your loss."

"*Danke.* I'm still in shock," said the girl and Hilde eyed her suspiciously.

Her suspicion grew only when the officer sang the praises of the late Obersturmbannführer Wolfgang Huber – Erika's father-in-law. Oh my God, that young lady couldn't be his daughter. It had been a while since she'd seen her at Erika's wedding, but she clearly remembered Annegret's high-pitched voice, which was in total contrast to the soft, subdued tone of this girl.

As soon as the officer left their compartment, Hilde accused the girl, "You're not Annegret Huber. Who are you?"

The girl's hand flew to her chest. "Of course I am."

Hilde shook her head at the girl's audacity. "You're lying."

"Why do you say that?" The Annegret impostor stared at her with pure terror in her eyes.

"I know Annegret, and you are not her."

The girl sagged and finally opened her mouth, "Look, the bombing today hit directly over the building in Nikolassee where I lived."

Hilde paled and grabbed her sleeping son tighter. She closed her eyes for a moment and prayed Q was okay. Even if her building had been hit, he could have been at work. He liked to work late. *Please. Please. Let him be fine.*

She gathered all her strength and forced out the words, "We live there. Where exactly was the hit?"

The young woman reached over to take her hand. "How horrible. Just about the whole block at the Rehwiese Park was flattened to the ground. Only the smaller buildings across the railway track weren't damaged."

Hilde sagged in relief and murmured, "Thank God."

"The alarms came too late, and most of the inhabitants didn't make it into the shelter. I was lucky because I got trapped under a broken staircase. Herr and Frau Huber, and Annegret, they're all dead."

"What is your real name?"

A long pause ensued before the girl finally answered. "Margarete Rosenbaum."

She's a Jew. That's why she's lying.

"All I want is to live." Tears pooled in Margarete's eyes, and she was barely able to form the words. "I was their maid for two years, but Herr Huber wanted to send me away by the end of the week."

Hilde had a good idea where a Jewish girl would have been sent. "Continue."

"I took Annegret's papers and then pinned the yellow star on her blouse. I just want to survive. Please."

Hilde didn't answer. Instead, she turned her head and looked out the window at the darkness beyond. *How far down can this country go?* A twenty-year-old girl had to assume someone else's identity in order to stay alive. This wasn't her country anymore.

She pondered whether she could help the girl but finally decided that the best she could do was to ignore everything that had happened during the last thirty minutes.

"I won't tell anyone," Hilde said and looked away again.

Volker awakened a little while later, and Hilde was thankful for the distraction. It was after dark when the train arrived in Magdeburg. As they stepped carefully down onto the platform, the girl helped her to unload her baggage and her son. Hilde met her eyes for a moment and said, "Good luck, Annegret."

Then she turned and stepped into the embrace of her sister Julia.

***

Initially, Hilde enjoyed her time on the farm with Julia. It was much more peaceful and relaxed than in the capital, but after a few days, she missed Q and her friends.

Julia had to work, like everyone else, and Hilde got increasingly lonely as the days turned into weeks. Hilde offered to help, but at seven months pregnant, she wasn't of much use with the hard work.

Volker wasn't much company either because he was now old enough to enjoy playing with the other children and the animals. The active little boy loved the animals, but he liked the hand carts even more. He would spend hours placing things into a hand cart and then pulling it around, like a toy wagon.

Hilde was happy that he was enjoying himself, but she longed for Q to arrive for Christmas.

"I'm so glad you're here," she said with tears in her eyes when she finally met him at the train station.

"I've missed you and Volker so much," he said, hugging and kissing her.

They celebrated Christmas with Julia, but nobody was in the mood to enjoy, except for Volker of course. Q was unusually distracted, and Hilde worried about him. Something had happened, but he wouldn't tell what it was.

When it was time for him to return to Berlin, she said, "I'm ready to come back with you."

"Hilde, I really think you should stay here until the baby is born."

"No! I won't have my baby so far away from you and my friends. Besides, I don't want to be alone any longer."

"It's safer here than in Berlin. You know that a big part of Nikolassee was reduced to rubble right after you left."

"I know, but I would rather die by your side than live without you."

He took her into his arms and whispered in her ear, "It's not yet time to die, Hildelein."

Q finally gave in, and right after New Year's they returned home. Despite knowing about the bomb damage to their quarter, she was still shocked to the core to see the sad remains of what used to be a thriving place.

One day, Hilde put Volker into his pram and walked to the building where Wolfgang Huber once lived. There wasn't much left of it. The entire building had collapsed in shambles, and only the back wall stood half intact.

An eerie cold seized her, and she sent a prayer to the sky, asking to keep Margarete safe before she hurried away.

Apart from that, things had returned to normal, if one could call this life normal. But something was off and the more time passed, the more certain Hilde became that Q was hiding something from her. She'd never seen him in such a state of anxious excitement, but whenever she asked him about it, he brushed it off. "I'm just worn out by the constant worry, and the raging war."

She could tell he was lying to her, but she didn't have the strength to confront him. With less than one month until the baby was due, she needed all her energy to keep her small family fed and keep Volker under control. The cute little man had developed into a little daredevil, and he missed the freedom of the countryside where he could play and run for hours on end.

She sighed. She wasn't entirely sure she wanted to know what Q was up to. In any case, a discussion with him would have to wait until the baby was born. Emma had agreed to stay with them for a month to help with Volker and the household chores, so Hilde could dedicate herself to the newborn.

Chapter 33

Q jumped up, and his chair fell back. "It's not possible!"

Martin, Erhard, and he had come up with and discarded idea after idea. Infiltrating a construction company and pretending to have to do maintenance work on the roof. Climbing up like a cat burglar. Landing with a makeshift parachute. Overwhelming the security guards. Getting security clearance for some of the buildings. They just couldn't get access to the roofs of those darn buildings.

Martin and Erhard looked at each other before they nodded. "It was a good idea, but we just can't get those blinking lights up on the roofs. All buildings of strategic importance are too closely guarded."

Q sighed with disappointment. "We had everything worked out. The production of the blinkers, the remote control, the radio transmitters, everything...but we can't get them up there."

Erhard put a hand on his shoulder. "Don't take it personally. We'll come up with another idea to torpedo the war effort."

Martin nodded. "Yes, we can make a change, we just need another idea."

The three men tossed around a few ideas over the next days, but nothing to be taken seriously. During their next quality control meeting, they discussed the radio transmitters for the Wehrmacht when Q suddenly said, "We'll make a remote controlled bomb."

The others looked at him with their jaws nearly on the floor. "A bomb? Sure we could do that, but why?"

Q suddenly knew exactly what he had to do. "To assassinate Hitler."

"To...what?" Martin drawled, the words barely making a sound.

"Yes. I will assassinate the Führer," Q reinforced.

"That would certainly solve some problems," Erhard said.

All three of them started tossing ideas around with ardent zeal. In moments, the disappointment over their failure to find a way to install the blinkers on the roofs was forgotten, and they outplayed each other with input for their newest project.

"We need to find a weakness...a time when he is less protected and vulnerable," Martin suggested.

They made a plan of action and distributed tasks. Erhard would feel out other resistance groups, and Martin would keep his eyes and ears open at the weekly Party meetings for any information they might use. Q was tasked to find out Hitler's daily routine.

Several weeks later, they had to abandon the idea of assassinating Hitler – he was too protected. Many before had tried, and nobody had ever succeeded. People outside his inner circle couldn't get close to the Führer anymore.

"What about Goebbels?" Erhard suggested. Goebbels was Minister of Propaganda and one of Hitler's most devoted followers. His excellent public speaking skills combined with a virulent anti-Semitism made him a dangerous weapon and an important pillar of Hitler's power.

"Goebbels?" Q asked. "If a more moderate person came into his position, that might lead to better conditions for the Jews and less support for the war amongst the civilians."

"Let's take the next week to think about it," Erhard suggested.

Q returned to the laboratory and started his daily work. For weeks, he'd been thinking about a way to shorten the war and speed up the tumbling of the

Thousand-Year Reich, should they have found the solution.

But could killing someone in cold blood be justified, even if done to save hundreds, maybe even thousands, of lives?

***

In March 1942, Hilde gave birth to her second baby, another son, and Q was proud as punch. He instantly fell in love with the cute little baby with a down of straight brown hair, much different from Volker's white-blond curly locks. But he shared the same blue eyes as his brother, and Q himself.

"Hilde, he looks exactly like you!" Q said.

She took a look at the baby's crumpled face and laughed. "I hope not." Then she stroked his tiny head with her palm and held him against her chest. "What shall we name him?"

"He looks like a Peter, doesn't he?"

"Peter? Well, I like it."

Q knew that Hilde had secretly hoped for a girl and had already chosen a girl's name, but for a boy they'd still been undecided between three or four options.

Emma, who had already arrived a few days ago, came into the bedroom with Volker holding her hand.

"I wanna see the baby!" Volker shouted and rushed toward the bed.

"Slow down!" Q scolded him. "Your brother, Peter, is very tiny and you will crush him with your weight."

Volker instantly looked guilty and slowed down his steps. Then he glanced at his mother with a questioning look in his eyes, and Q saw how a warm smile spread across her face as she nodded. Volker crawled onto the bed and carefully caressed his baby brother's hand.

Q's heart constricted, seeing the three of them like that, happy and united in love. He couldn't – no, he wouldn't – be responsible for tearing them apart. Something had to give.

Emma put a hand on his arm and said, "We should take a picture of them."

He nodded and went to his study to retrieve the photo camera to capture this moment of love.

***

The weeks went by, and the more Q thought about the planned assassination attempt, the more worried he became. Not for himself, but for Hilde and the boys. The possibility of destroying their happiness lay hard on his conscience, so hard that one day he decided to visit his mother.

"Wilhelm, what a surprise," Ingrid said as she opened the door for him.

Q fidgeted with his hands. "Hello, Mother. Can I come in.?"

"Sure, my darling. But what brings you here, in plain daylight on a workday? Is everything fine with Hilde and the boys?"

"Yes." He didn't know what else to say. *They're fine for now, but soon their lives might be torn to pieces – because of me.*

His mother smiled. "I'm getting old. The last time all of you visited, I had to sit in my armchair the rest of the day and relax. Volker sure is a handful, but Peter is such a sweet and content baby. They're so different from each other."

"Mother…" He looked at the woman he'd loved his entire life and longed to tell her the truth.

"Son, I'll make us an infusion." She led him to the tiny kitchen and made an herb tea. "I'm sorry, I don't have coffee."

"Nobody has real coffee anymore…" Q sat down and stared at his mother's back, while she boiled water. He wasn't sure why he'd come here. She wouldn't be able to help. Nobody could.

Ingrid carried two steaming cups and sat down at the kitchen table with Q. "What do you have on your heart?"

The burden of his conscience weighed him down, and he couldn't look into his mother's eyes as he handed her an envelope stuffed with money. "Will you keep this for me? If anything happens..." He couldn't bring himself to finish the sentence.

His mother put her hand under his chin and raised his head to look into his eyes. She would be able to see right into his soul, like she always had. Now she would scold him for being such a foolish and egotistic man. But she didn't.

After a long time, she said, "Wilhelm, I'm worried about you. You've always been a free thinker, but these are not the times to play hero. Whatever you are up to, I don't want to know about it. But promise me one thing...be careful."

He nodded. "I will."

She kissed his forehead and took the envelope. "I'll guard this until you come and take it back."

"Thank you, Mother. I love you." He rushed out to hide his glistening eyes. *Damn! Damn! Damn!*

A few weeks later, Q came up with the perfect solution to protect Hilde and the boys in case he was found out.

One night when the kids were asleep, he took Hilde's hand and led her to the couch. "Hilde, I want you to hear me out. Things are getting more dangerous, and I worry about you and the boys. I need to keep you safe."

She made a face.

"If we are no longer together, nobody will hold you responsible for my actions."

"What?" she demanded, her eyes wide open with shock.

"We'll feign a fight, and you will leave. Take the kids someplace safe where my actions won't reflect on you."

"Absolutely not! There's no way I'll do that. Without you, I might as well die right now." She jumped from the couch and stared at him, her hands resting on her hips.

"Hilde, please be reasonable. If you can't think about yourself, think about the children."

"My answer is no. This discussion is over." Turning on her heel, Hilde took herself off to bed.

The next morning before he had to leave for work, he brought the subject up again. "Hilde, just say you'll think about it," he pleaded with her.

But she was adamant. "I will not! Nothing will make me change my mind about this. We are a family, and we will stay together until they force us apart. Full stop."

This went on for a few days, until he finally relented. "Fine. We'll stay together."

For the first time since he'd brought up the topic, she smiled at him. "Finally, you're coming to your senses."

Chapter 34

Hilde put two mugs of ersatz coffee on the breakfast table and watched her sleepy husband as he took a big gulp. "God, how I hate this *Muckefuck!* Isn't there real coffee to be had anywhere?"

She hid her smile at his outburst and took a sip of her own, then grimaced. "I don't know why I still drink that stuff. Maybe we should instead try one of the suggestions from the propaganda ministry."

Q looked at her and raised a brow, "What?"

"They now want us to use common weeds as food."

"Weeds? You can't be serious." He put down his mug. "Although I'm not sure anything can be worse than this. If we at least had sugar…"

"See here." She showed him a leaflet that had been distributed to all households and summarized the contents. "The solution to our malnutrition apparently is growing along the roadsides and in the wooded areas. Here's a recipe to make a salad of stinging nettle, common dandelions, and cabbage thistle. Ugh." Hilde put the leaflet down and grimaced.

Q grinned at her. "Hmm, I can see the children running to the table for their share of stinging nettle. Any more pearls of wisdom in there?"

She scanned the leaflet and shook her head. "Not much. They advise the good German housewife to collect those 'nutritious herbs' along the sides of the road to prepare a healthy meal for our families. Apparently, those adjustments to our diet will help us live even better and healthier than before the war."

"Well, then let's take a walk along the Autobahn and see if we can find us a good lunch."

Hilde tossed the leaflet onto the table in disgust. "What a load of bullshit!"

Her outburst caused a laugh to spring from Q's lips. Normally she was much better at controlling her response. But the war and the constant threat of being discovered had frayed her nerves.

Q sighed, running a hand through his hair. "This is the price we have to pay for Hitler's delusions of grandeur. I'd dispose of him if I could."

His remark was casual, but Hilde was shocked nonetheless. *Would Q actually kill the man, given the chance?*

Her heart constricted. Suddenly his strange behavior, the need to get rid of her and the children, everything fell into place like a jigsaw.

She took a deep breath to calm her racing heart, but she didn't dare ask. She wasn't even sure she wanted to know.

***

Germany was in the middle of the worst war in the history of mankind, but the Nazi regime failed to acknowledge the hardships for the civilians and touted their war successes. According to the media and leaflets, everyone not willing to suffer for their leader was a traitor to the nation and should be treated as such.

Hilde often stood for hours in line to buy food or clothing. Keeping an entire family well fed wasn't an easy task, and she was grateful that she had enough milk to nurse Peter. One less problem that weighed down on her shoulders.

Peter was such a content baby, and Hilde barely noticed his presence. He would be happy to play with an old piece of cloth and lie in his crib babbling at himself. He'd even sleep through the frequent trips to the bomb shelter, and she'd often joke with Q that you could literally drop a bomb beside his head without waking him.

Volker, on the other hand, had become a handful and hard to manage. He was very intelligent for his age and more curious than was good for him. He kept Hilde on her toes around the clock. During the day, he ventured out, and at night, he was plagued by nightmares.

The trips to the shelter were something he abhorred and feared. Almost every night, she had to drag a crying toddler down into the cellar. But what else could she do? He was too young to understand and too old not to understand.

Q helped her as much as he could, but as the war wore on, everyone was required to work overtime and put in weekends. Vacation was a word of the past. And to be honest, what would they do during vacation?

Hilde sighed and put down her needlework. She'd resorted to mending and re-mending Volker's clothes, attaching pieces of textile to make the pants and shirts cover his growing legs and arms. Right then, she was cutting up an old skirt of hers and making it into matching shirts for the boys.

When would this end? Desperation took hold of her, and she shed a few tears.

On Sunday, Leopold Stieber and his wife came over to visit with their children. Hilde offered them some bread and herb tea.

When Dörthe saw the green liquid, she raised her brow. "You're not picking weeds at the side of the street, are you?"

Hilde laughed. "I wouldn't. They could as well ask us to sweep up the dust on the streets and stretch the flour with it."

Dörthe grimaced. "Ugh."

"No, I grew lemon balm and peppermint on the windowsill."

Leopold and Q joined their discussion, and soon they were telling jokes about the bad conditions.

Leopold said, "This one is good: Someone tried to commit suicide by hanging himself, only the rope had been made with such poor quality material, it couldn't withstand his weight and broke.

"He then tried to drown himself in the river, but the suit he was wearing contained too much wood, and he ended up floating and couldn't make himself sink.

"Despondent, he returned home and went back to living and eating only the official rations the government gave him. He was dead two months later."

Everyone shared a laugh; it was better than crying in despair. Only Dörthe sent her husband a scathing glance. "You should know better than to tell such a joke. We could all be sent to prison."

"Come on, Dörthe, we do need to have some fun."

The Stiebers soon left and the daily routine returned. Hilde made it a habit to take turns visiting her mother-in-law and her own mother. She also took many pictures of the boys and regularly sent letters to Emma and Carl.

Her relationship with her mother had steadily improved over the last year. Hilde had finally accepted Annie's selfish nature and tried to not let it bother her.

Her mother seemed to make an effort to change, and she was always excited to see the boys – for a short while. Volker's explorative spirit and Annie's immaculate apartment didn't mesh well.

"I can hold the baby for you. You keep Volker away from my glassware."

Hilde sighed and handed Peter to his grandmother. Some things would never change. Peter seemed to be quite taken with his grandmother and soaked her blouse in baby drool, which earned him a sour face but no complaint.

Meanwhile, Volker tried to discover how fast he could run from one end of the living room to the other, cheering himself on and clapping his hands after each turn.

"He's much too wild," Annie complained, and Hilde tried to distract him with a picture book she'd brought along.

When Peter began to fuss, Hilde said, "I'll take him back, he must be hungry."

As she began to nurse him, her mother gave her a disgusted glance. "You shouldn't be doing that. It's not ladylike. It would be better to give him a bottle."

"I disagree, besides the milk is bad, even when it's available. How can you feed an infant only skim milk?"

Annie retreated into the kitchen, and it soon started smelling heavenly. She returned a few minutes later with two cups of coffee. Real coffee.

Hilde finished nursing Peter and then laid him against her shoulder. "Oh my God, Mother, where did you get real coffee?"

But her mother chose not to answer, and instead, sipped at the cup. "It's good, isn't it?"

It was.

The full aroma of sweet and fruity coffee with just a hint of pleasant bitterness exploded on Hilde's taste buds. "Hmm. Wonderful."

A few minutes later, Hilde said, "In the tram, I overheard a conversation. Their neighbor got caught trying to stockpile food from a farmer and has been sent to one of the labor camps."

Annie nodded. "Well done. *Im Krieg ist sparen Deine Pflicht.*"

Hilde raised a brow at her mother's attitude. "Do you really believe it is your duty to skimp because we are at war?"

"Yes. It's also a crime against the Fatherland to keep more rations than someone is assigned."

"Says the woman who has real coffee in her home," Hilde responded, unable to keep the bitterness from her tone.

Annie shrugged, not looking the least bit embarrassed. "My husband is a famous opera singer. I can't well decline if people want to show their appreciation for his talents."

"Did you know that people are actually killed in those so-called labor camps? Especially those in Poland?"

"Those are just silly rumors." Annie sat down her empty cup and waved her hand, as if she could wave away the truth so easily.

"Are they?"

"Does it matter if they're true? The Jews deserve it for ruining Germany. The least they can do is work to help bring her back to her former glory."

"Mother, they're being killed." Hilde scowled.

"I don't believe that for a minute." Her mother stood up and looked at the clock on the bureau. "I'm afraid I have to leave now. Robert is singing tonight at the State Opera."

"Well, give him my best wishes. I'll come by next week again." On her way home, Hilde pondered over the fate of those deported to one of the labor camps. She hadn't believed the news when Q first brought it to her attention. But he'd sworn it was true; it had reached him through some secret channels from someone working for the Polish resistance.

But all the signs pointed to it being the truth. No one had ever come back to tell. She remembered the young woman she'd met on the train to Magdeburg. SS-Obersturmbannführer Huber's maid. Why was she so afraid, if she didn't have inside knowledge? Something only a few initiated knew about.

Chapter 35

Q spent many sleepless nights and anguished days arguing with his conscience. He was a pacifist and had always prided himself to believe in the good of mankind.

But in light of the atrocities the regime had committed and continued to commit, he felt the urge to change the course of history.

He wrote in his diary…

Is one human life worth more than another one? Is one life worth less than a thousand? Who am I to take the decision out of God's hand of who should live and who shouldn't?

Is it my mission to go against the basic rules of mankind and murder one person to try and save thousands?

Am I any better than the worst of the Nazi followers if I raise my hand against a fellow human?

No, the die is cast, and I should not waver in my faith to do the right thing. I believe the Gods have put me onto this world for a reason.

If I do not survive, I'm consoled by the fact that I always acted in good faith. I hope my children and history will one day forgive my deeds and see them for what they are: a desperate attempt to turn the wheel around for a world worth living in.

Q closed the diary and hid it on the top shelf in his study. Then he went to work. Summer was in full bloom, the blossoming chestnut trees a stark contrast to the burnt buildings lining the streets of Berlin. No major street had gone unscathed by the continuous bombings.

Martin and Erhard already waited for him. During the last weeks and months, they had meticulously worked on their assassination plan, adding detail after detail. Coming up with an idea, only to discard it when they gathered the next piece of information about Goebbels.

They had investigated everything about him. His daily routine. His office. His home. His family. His travels. The people he spent time with. Finally, everything began to fall into place, and their plan was slowly taking shape.

"His office is too closely guarded," Erhard said.

"But we don't want to harm his family, so his house is out of the question," Martin said and then added, "have you seen where he lives?"

"No." The other two shook their heads in unison. Martin had been tasked with that part of the operation, and as a devoted Party member, he'd even managed to get an invite to one of the pompous parties Goebbels liked to host.

"He has bought the estates of two exiled Jewish bank directors and joined the properties. The mansion he's built to replace the two former ones is simply outstanding."

"We wouldn't get inside anyways," Q cautioned and rubbed his chin. "He lives on that upper-class island Schwanenwerder in the Wannsee, right?"

Martin nodded, and Q continued, "I live not too far away from there. We used to take bicycle tours along the Wannsee. As far as I know, there's only one bridge connecting the island with the mainland. The Schwanenwerder Bridge."

"I know that bridge. There's not much traffic, only inhabitants are allowed on the island nowadays," Erhard said.

Martin agreed. "He has to cross that bridge every morning and every evening. It's the perfect place to plant our bomb."

"We have to think about it," Q said, and everyone agreed. They decided that Q should have a look at the bridge on the weekend since he lived the closest to it. They would meet the following week to discuss further steps.

Back at home, Q wanted to tell Hilde what he was up to. He opened his mouth several times to explain, but no words came out. Whenever he looked into her trusting blue eyes, his throat went dry.

No, he just couldn't bring himself to destroy the little piece of mind she still had.

Always in tune with her husband, Hilde picked up on his worries. "What's wrong, my love. You've been incredibly tense these last weeks."

He sighed. "I am. All of this anxiety is taking a toll on me. But I don't want to bother you with it, you have your hands full with the boys."

Hilde intensely studied his face, and he forced himself not to flinch. "We should go for a walk to the Wannsee beach on the weekend, it will help to get your mind off whatever troubles you."

Hell no! "That's a good idea. We have to hold onto what little happiness we have left in these dark days," Q answered and felt like a traitor. How could he concentrate on his family when the potential crime scene lay in plain sight? On the other hand, it would be the perfect excuse to take a closer look at the Schwanenwerder Bridge.

The next Monday, Q returned to Loewe and his partners in crime with a plan. The small wooden bridge was the perfect target.

"We can plant our bomb beneath the bridge, and I'll detonate when Goebbels Mercedes passes over," Q explained.

"We have to find out the times he passes over the bridge and set a timer," Erhard said.

"No, that's too hit-or-miss. I'll wait nearby and trigger the remote control right when the car rolls over the bomb. Because the bridge is so old, cars have to go slow. It will be easy to identify the exact moment."

Martin shook his head. "I don't like it. It's too dangerous. If someone sees you—"

"This is the crux. I initially wanted to hide behind the trees, but that's too suspicious. I need a legitimate reason to linger near the bridge, maybe for hours..."

Erhard jumped up and shouted, "Fishing!"

"What?" Q asked, quite puzzled upon the sudden outburst of his friend.

"Fishing. You disguise yourself as a fisherman and wait on a boat in the water with the fishing rod in hand a short distance away from the bridge."

"That's a fantastic idea. That will work," Martin chimed in, and even Q had to agree that this definitely could work. "Now we only need to secure the boat and the fishing equipment."

"It's a deal then," Erhard stated. "Let's start building our bomb."

Building the bomb was the easy part because they could tap into the resources at Loewe. Martin was tasked with building the bomb itself while Q and his wireless equipment department handled the remote control unit. His employees, of course, thought they were working on a new prototype for the *Wehrmacht.*

It took Q plenty of time and a considerable amount of effort and money before he was able to source the boat and fishing equipment.

Once the equipment was in place, they just had to determine at which times Goebbels would most likely cross the bridge. Martin and Q worked out a schedule so that they could take turns observing their target.

Chapter 36

Q was waiting for his tram to arrive when a teenage boy joined him at the tram stop.

"Are you Herr Quedlin?" the boy asked.

"Yes." Q nodded, wondering what he could want.

"I have a message for you. Open on page seven." With these words, the boy handed him a newspaper and quickly disappeared around the corner.

Q's curiosity was spiked, but he didn't dare open the paper in plain sight. Instead, he meticulously folded it twice and stored it in his briefcase. Only when he was home, in the safe confinement of his study, did his shaky fingers find page seven.

He gasped. A note lay inside: *Meet tomorrow at six p.m. at Westkreuz train station. Bring your half of the torn map.*

His heart raced. Q hadn't heard anything from Moscow since Pavel had left Berlin more than a year ago. Communication was difficult these days, and from Erhard, he knew that the other resistance groups also had trouble staying in touch.

What if this was a trap? He retrieved his half from his desk and scrutinized it carefully. Could anyone have known about the map?

Hilde called out to him. "Q, dinner is ready." He stored the map and the note in his briefcase and exited his study to have dinner with his family.

Later that evening, he told Hilde about the note he'd received.

"If this was a trap, how would they know about you and the map the Russian agent gave you?" she asked.

"The Gestapo has means to get everyone to talk." He shuddered, remembering the horror stories he'd heard.

She put a hand on his arm. "This may be so. But I believe the Gestapo wouldn't go to so much trouble if they wanted to arrest you. They'd burst in here and haul you away."

A shiver of fear ran down his spine. "You're right. I will go to the meeting place."

The next day he was sitting on pins and needles, unable to concentrate on his work. More than once, he opened his briefcase to feel the map tucked away inside a newspaper. The hands on the clock in the laboratory moved excruciatingly slow until it was finally time to leave.

Q arrived at Westkreuz Station, which was crowded with workers on their way home. As if by magic, a man appeared and asked if he had a map of Berlin. *This must be my contact.* Cold sweat broke out on Q's forehead. Unlike the other agents he'd met, this one clearly was German and not Russian. Q barely remembered the question he was supposed to ask.

"Is the hike up Mount Etna strenuous, *mein Herr*?"

The man looked confused and then laughed. "Not at all. Only if you intend it at night. Didn't you trust the map, comrade?"

Relief flooded his entire body, and Q shook the agent's extended hand. "Never can be too careful, comrade. Can I see the map, please?"

They sat on one of the waiting benches, and the agent handed him a newspaper with the map inside. Q laid it beside his own. They fit perfectly.

"Satisfied?" When Q nodded, the agent introduced himself. "Gerald Meier, Wehrmacht deserter and proud member of the Red Army."

"You probably already know who I am," Q said and leaned back to watch a few pigeons fighting for crumbs. Before the war, old men and women had come here to feed the birds, but nowadays nobody had food to spare.

"I thought all agents had been recalled. How did you get back into Germany?" Q asked.

"That's quite a story. Care to take a ride?"

Q nodded, and they jumped on the next suburban train. Gerald gestured to keep silent until they reached their destination. After a fifteen-minute ride, they got off at one of the deserted suburban stations that only saw crowds twice a day.

They found another waiting bench and sat down. "I parachuted into Sweden about a month ago and made my way down here," Gerald said. "Because I'm German, I've had no problem getting along, and I've been living in Berlin with some old friends."

Gerald Meier probably wasn't his real name, if he really was a Wehrmacht deserter.

"How do you make contact with Moscow?" Q asked.

"I have a transmitter."

"Why me?"

"My superiors gave me a list of contacts I should try and re-activate. Pavel was sure you'd still be on our side. Is that so?"

Q nodded. "My opinions haven't changed. In fact…"

"In fact, what?"

"Nothing. What kind of information do you need?"

Gerald squinted his eyes and looked sharply at Q before nodding. "Basically everything you can give us. Headquarters will decide whether it's important for their strategy or not. A summary of production at Loewe would be a good start. Together with blueprints for any and all new advances you've made in the last year. Especially wireless transmission, echo-sound, and this new radar thing everyone raves about."

"I can do this, but it will take some time. A week at least."

"Fine, meet me a week from now. Same place same time." With a nod, Gerald stood and walked away.

Q was left alone in a deserted train station with plenty of information to think about. He would have a lot of work to do.

Chapter 37

Hilde had just put the boys to bed when she heard the door.

"You're late, Q. I was worried."

He took her into his arms. "I'm sorry. I wish someone would invent a telephone that we can always carry with us. Then I could have advised you."

Hilde laughed. "How would that work? Should we always drag along a cable reel? Maybe loop it around our necks."

"No, it would need to work without a cable." He furrowed his brows and crossed his arms over his chest. "In fact, a few years back, the Canadian David Hings invented a portable two-way radio and called it a Walkie-Talkie. The problem with those Walkie-Talkies is that their range is very limited, and they work even less reliably in a city with many buildings, but I might be able to–"

"Q, you digress. Tell me about the meeting with that...man."

Q relayed what happened, closing with, "I have to replicate as many technical instructions as possible until next week."

"I could help," she offered.

"You? No way. I'm not dragging you into this." He plopped on the couch. "Is there dinner left for me?"

Hilde smiled. "Yes, I kept it warm for you. And nice change of topic."

"You know me too well." Q smirked. "But I am hungry."

"Fine. I'll set the table for you."

Hilde thought this was the end of the discussion. Since the birth of Peter, Q had been overly protective and had tried to keep her away from his resistance work. It was a wonder he'd told her about the Russian agent.

She frowned at the memory of his hilarious suggestion to make her leave after a feigned fight. *Over my dead body.* An icy shiver ran down her spine, and she pushed the foreboding away. There wouldn't be any dead bodies. Not hers. Not Q's. Not anyone's.

But three days later, Q came home from work with a pile of papers and asked her to typewrite them later in the evening.

Hilde eyed them suspiciously. "What's this?"

"Just some technical stuff," he said without going into further detail.

But Hilde knew.

She retrieved the children and seated them at the table for dinner. Q's face shone with pride as he looked at his sons. While Volker was the spitting image of his father, Peter took after his mother. Barely six months old, he was already sitting at the table with them and eating the same, albeit mashed up, food.

After dinner, Q read a book to Volker while Hilde rocked Peter to sleep on her lap. When both children were sound asleep, Q and Hilde retreated to his study.

She'd often done the writing and copying for him, and sat down at the typewriter, ready to have him dictate the technical texts to her.

"No, wait," he said. "I want you to layer several papers on top of each other."

Hilde observed him layering white paper, blueprint paper, and brown paper before he handed her the pile. "Here, put this into the machine."

"Why do I need to do this? We haven't done it this way before."

"Hilde, I just want to try it this way. Besides, it's better that you don't know everything. You need to be able to say you had no knowledge about the technical stuff you were typing."

She exhaled a long breath. "Fine. Let's start." *I bet this has to do with meeting that Russian agent.*

When she had filled the paper, she took it out, removed the white paper from the pile, and replaced it with a new one. The letters on the white paper were slightly smeared, but still legible. *Why did he want the letters to be smeared?*

Chapter 38

Q now met with Gerald on a weekly basis. Together with Erhard and Martin, he handed him all the intelligence they could possibly gather, not only from Loewe but also from every source they had access to. Erhard and Q were still active members of several scientific circles, and Martin often got hold of classified material via his Party connections.

Gerald always praised the good quality of the information, and more than once, brought back a message from Moscow on how much they appreciated the detailed intelligence about position finder beacons, a bomb that automatically steered according to light, and even a technical paper on the use of hydrogen peroxide to propel torpedoes of V-weapons – weapons of retaliation.

"Do you think this will help to shorten the war?" Q asked.

Gerald tried to say something uplifting but then shook his head. "I'm afraid not. Despite the messages of endurance from the official channels, there's nothing that gives me new hope. The Wehrmacht is overrunning our Red Army, and I'm afraid Russia is in danger of losing the battle of Stalingrad."

On the next meeting, Gerald was strangely withdrawn. He avoided eye contact with Q and even stopped joking about the pep talks from his superiors.

"Something wrong?" Q asked him.

Gerald squirmed. "No. Everything is all right, I guess all the tension is taking a toll on me."

"Me too? You have no idea how often I wanted to jump ship."

"No. Now's not the time. We might be getting closer to victory."

Q doubted that, but he had an ace up his sleeve: the assassination attempt of Goebbels. It had to happen soon because winter was coming and the Wannsee might freeze up. Preparations had been ongoing throughout summer, and despite various setbacks and postponements, they had finally settled on a date. December 1st 1942.

He knew he was playing a dangerous game and wanted to get it over with before he met Gerald again. Then he'd be able to bring some good news. *I hope.*

"I think we should wait and not meet again until December. I'm swamped with work and can't give you much useful info at the moment."

Gerald flinched. "No, we have to meet before that. Moscow depends on your intel. We're so close to making progress in the battle of Stalingrad."

"Fine." Q sighed. "Give me at least two weeks and let's meet at the end of the month." It would be two days before the assassination and might even give him a small reprieve to have something else to think about.

That night, Q returned home and dropped a bomb on his wife. "We're going to assassinate Goebbels."

Hilde swayed and held on to the table before plopping down on her chair. She gulped several times. "You're serious, aren't you?"

"Dead serious."

A nervous giggle escaped her mouth. "Why you?"

Q stroked her head. "It has to be done, and I'm in the best position to do it."

They sat on the couch into the wee hours of the night, holding onto one another. Hilde whispered, "Two weeks. I'm afraid."

"I'm afraid too. But I have Martin and Erhard covering for me. Nobody will ever know I was near that bridge."

Martin would help him attach the bomb the day before the planned attack, and he would cover for him at Loewe while Q was sitting on the water in his boat waiting for Goebbels's limousine to cross the bridge.

Hilde trembled in his arms. "Please calm down," he urged her when she started to cry. "Tell me what you've done this week."

Hilde dried her tears. "I started weaning Peter. He's such a big boy now and eats so well with us. It's a bit sad but will give me more independence."

Q hugged her. "Yes, our baby is growing rapidly. And Volker, he's such an intelligent boy. When this war is over, we might add a little girl to our family, what do you think?"

She leaned against him and laughed. "With our luck, it will be a third boy."

"Doesn't matter. Let's go to bed and practice."

As they passed the nursery, Hilde disappeared inside to give them a kiss and then returned with a winter coat in her hands.

"I finished this today. I made it for Volker from one of your old jackets. Now he will at least have a memory of you if you should die."

Q took her into his arms and promised to take every precaution. "Even if I get caught, there's nothing they can hold against you. Remember that. I will love you for eternity."

He took her to their bedroom and made sweet love to her, holding her afterwards until the sun rose over the horizon.

Chapter 39

The days crawled by at a snail's pace as Q prepared for the assassination. Everything was finished, and all they had to do was wait.

Meeting Gerald was a welcome distraction from Q's anxiety. He didn't have much to report because his thoughts had been focused solely on the attack. But still, he'd managed to copy a few construction drawings.

Q arrived at *Potsdamer Platz* by underground and surfaced onto the square. The November wind chilled his bones and fog wafted across the vast square.

As he approached the meeting spot on the stairs leading up to the train station, he was suddenly surrounded by Gestapo officers. *"Halt!* You're arrested."

Q's heart sank. Did they mean him? He looked around, seeing no sign of Gerald, only six Gestapo officers bearing down on him. His pulse raced, and despite the cold, sweat formed on his forehead. "Is there a problem, officers?"

"Put your hands up! You are arrested for crimes against Germany and the Party."

Q did as he was asked, putting up no resistance as two officers grabbed him rather roughly and dragged him to a waiting car. They pushed him inside, and the car took off with him and the three Gestapo men inside.

"What have I done?" Q asked, trying to keep the fear and nerves out of his voice.

The senior officer looked at him and sneered, "You will be informed of the charges against you, but not here. You are coming with us."

Q sent up a silent prayer to the Gods above to keep his family safe. The image of Hilde holding Peter in her arms, with Volker standing by her side as he left this morning, filled his mind.

I love you, my darlings!

After ten years of spying and trying to bring down the regime, he'd finally been caught.

It is over.

***

As you may imagine, Q's resistance work may be over, but there's still much more to his story. Book 3 will be about his time in prison, and also tell you what happened to Hilde and her two sons.

Coming soon..... CLICK HERE to get an email reminder as soon as book 3 is released and to receive exclusive background material about the true story behind this book.

Thank you for taking the time to read UNYIELDING. If you enjoyed it, please consider telling your friends or posting a short review. Word of mouth is an author's best friend.

Thank you,

Acknowledgements

First of all I want to thank all my fantastic readers who've given me personal feedback or reviewed my first book Unrelenting. Without your encouragement I wouldn't have persisted to write part 2 and part 3 (in the works).

My terrific cover designer Daniela from www.stunningbookcovers.com, has once again taken my ideas and made them into a wonderful cover, that – in my opinion – captures exactly the mood of the book and the times back then.

And a book could never be complete without a thorough editor. Lynette Patterson has once again provided immensely helpful advice for the first draft, as well as found a thousand and one typos in the finished manuscript.

Many thanks also to JJ Toner who thoroughly checked and proofread my manuscript.

Contact Me & Other Books

I truly appreciate you taking the time to read (and enjoy) my books. And I'd be thrilled to hear from you!

If you'd like to get in touch with me you can do so via

Twitter:

http://twitter.com/MarionKummerow

Facebook:

http://www.facebook.com/AutorinKummerow

Website

http://www.kummerow.info

Other books written by Marion Kummerow:

http://kummerow.info/my-books